Waiting Fo

by

Stephensor

www.stephensonholt.com

contact@stephensonholt.com

@HoltStephenson

Dedication.

The Welsh verb "Dysgu" means both to learn and to teach. It suggests a transfer of information. This book is dedicated to four children who have not only learnt from me but have taught me even more; to see life with a blank canvas, with no pre-conceived ideas, to observe everything around me and to use my imagination to the full.

How many times are you going to fly

Down that slippery slide, until you decide

That it's much more fun to turn back and run

From bottom to top, until, that forced stop

Where you fall on your face and without real pace

You giggle right back to the bottom?

We return to our car at the dirt-windowed house

Did they die (far less mirth) are they now in the earth

We scrump through their brambles one eye on their door

The juice from the berries drips hand-mouth to floor

No sharks live by us Bampa, so you'll never die

But if this did happen, I don't think I'll cry but say

Wow, how did that just happen?

Chapter 1

The sloped clearing in the Cornish oak-wood, bathed in dappled sunlight, had looked preferable to the muscle sapping mud of the pathway and Rebecca had decided to rest there under the soft light that was diffused by the summer tree canopy and that almost forced her to further postpone her random search for a murdering rapist. The bluebells around her, polka-dotted their brown paper back-drop of last year's dried-dead oak leaves and, even though not at their freshest, the perfume from each delicate bell was still inviting insects from outside the wood to enter in. Her head was lowered almost to ground level except for the rucksack pillow and was conveniently at the same height as the feeding insects and she watched the combined weight of a bee and a bell bending the stretched-thin stem that was previously reaching up towards the light. Her rest was coming to an end. The oak leaf bed had been a trap and hid a layer of sponge-damp leaf mould underneath it. The moisture had penetrated her cargo trousers and her sensible pants and now she felt it wetting her bum.

The part of her brain that was arguing against rising out of the damp was being led by forest-drowsiness from heady bluebell perfumes and it was easy for her to imagine how fairy stories were born in such places. The muted pastel shades of leaf greens and many varieties of bluebell blues had relaxed her eyes and made her sleepy, the only sounds to be heard, that of occasional high-pitched bird song penetrating the bass drone of the bees. Rebecca felt rested but a feeling of guilt was urging her journey on, amplified by the digging into her right thigh, between hip and knee, of the pistol that she had obtained from the old Cretan goat herder who had priced it at three hundred euros or an hour of sex and was now in her pocket.

Her mind jolted into the present with a speedy flash of blue, as the adult bird returned to the hole in the oak tree with a caterpillar in its beak and she wanted that photo of the twt-tomos-las, or whatever it was called in English, (she knew but couldn't remember) that photo of the chick sticking out its head from the nest hole and its even bigger beak begging for food but she should have been aimlessly wandering the countryside as lives possibly depended on that wandering. She knew that none of her photos would be in focus or unspoiled by movement, that she was too low down to get the right angle and that she couldn't send them to her photo agency, but hey, it was a rest, surely she deserved a rest and who would know anyway. The woods were too dark for decent shots with such a long lens and, even though it was summer, it had already started to smell like autumn here, the wet earth having the distinct earthy odour, much beloved by red wine experts with their flowery descriptions.

She was being paid a small day-rate, along with others, to carry out unofficial work and not to photograph nature, but she loved it, both the photography and the nature. Photography provided an even playing field for once, where photographs were judged on their merit, where nobody could tell, or care, whether a photo had been taken by a man or a woman and equality and feminist principles ruled supreme. As she looked upward through the shards of light, she realised that this would be a day of bright sunshine on the other side of this Celtic forest and the similarity with Dinas Wood and the pied flycatchers of Mid-Wales, all those years ago, was not lost on her. She hoped that when she reached the bright sun it would be warm enough to dry the, probably embarrassing, wet patch covering her bum without leaving too much of a stain. Her wet back, drying nicely as she stood and flapped the back of her loose lumberjack shirt to let the drying air in, would soon be wet again as the heavy rucksack clung tightly to her spine. The baseball cap, with water stains on it from sweat, received again her pushed in sandy, shoulder length mop making her look even more boyish, as if three weeks of camping with no makeup could make that much of a difference. It was time to get on with things, to look for anything slightly suspicious like a freshly dug grave or scattered female clothing.

As Rebecca stepped out of the low light of the oak forest she shielded her eyes as she was almost blinded by the sun hitting the morning dew and a million tiny mirrors on the short grass as the sun stretched itself to reach this side of the oak trees but failed. She gave a short intake of breath and held it as she looked down the steep field, dotted with sheep that were busy grazing on luscious grass and oblivious to the scene being played out, even further down the hill, below them and below Rebecca.

She was forced to stand and analyse the situation for a minute and hope that she wouldn't be accused, not for the first time, of exaggerating an innocent scenario. In the past she'd been guilty of making up stories that just weren't happening in reality and, this time, her eyes were also adjusting to the bright light after the dark of the woods and she was still squinting. As far as she could make out, far below her a man was panting and probably sweating in the heat as he furiously dug a trench, a trench shielded from the road by a high hedge, near the gate of the sheep's field where his van obscured a view into the field and it could be innocent enough, but from the detailed information she'd been given weeks earlier she wondered if the rolled up carpet next to the ditch may well be something of significance. Before stopping to photograph the birds on the woodland hilltop path, the very detailed map on her handheld satnav had told her that once she exited the woodland, there would be a steep downward slope, with a non-defined path around the edge of a field, down to a country lane, but it had not readied her for what she was now looking at.

Her mind raced and then froze, making for her the decision to procrastinate and not call anyone to give them her story until she was more certain of what was happening and when she was surer that this wasn't the unlikely scenario of a farmer digging a runner bean trench in a sheep field and using the carpet for moisture retention underneath the bean's roots. She checked her phone though, established that she did have a signal and carried on looking, unobserved, at what was happening below her, wondering why, if her worse case scenario was correct, that this should be happening in broad daylight and not under cover of darkness.

Searching for the correct course of action, eventually thinking back to her very minimal training, she decided she should walk down towards the man and his parked van, inwardly talk to herself about everything that she could see and hear to log it into her memory bank, ready for possible recall at a later date and to have the camera, that was still around her neck, switched back onto the 'on' position with the long, fifty to five hundred millimetre zoom lens ready with the lens cap most definitely off. Thankfully, her longest lens was already on her camera because... *Blue tit, got it, twt-tomos-las, blue tomos tit, blue tit. My memory is not as bad as I thought it was! Isn't it strange how these things come back to you when you're thinking about something else?'*

In a life changing moment, the DVD showing the highlights of her whole day went into fast-forward. The rolled up carpet, a nineteen eighties pattern that she recognised from who knows where, still at a great distance from her, appeared to move slightly and Rebecca wondered if her three week long camping and walking mission might be coming to a conclusion. She was definitely not exaggerating what was happening down there and an instant but calmly calculated and educated decision was needed and needed from her now this minute. With the cover of the trees behind her, the time it took to make five quick photos of the whole scene, a hundred metres away, and then zoom in to the man and his spade, gave her enough time to make that decision which was, extremely stupidly, to run down the hill like a wild thing, shouting at the top of her voice and waving her arms like a windmill.

"Hey, hey, thank God I've found someone. I've been lost for days, scared stiff, help me, please, help me."

She knew the words weren't believable before they came out of her mouth. It was a rubbish plan and she wanted to pause, press rewind, think of something smart and clever and start again but it was too late to change. It was impossible to stop and her body, being in a downhill motion, would eventually reach its target, like it or not. She wondered, briefly, what she would do if the man possessed a firearm. She readied herself to hit the floor and get behind a sheep, but that would be a last resort so she blocked that from her mind and started to concentrate on moving forward without hitting one of the still-static, still munching on grass, sheep and also to worry about the state of her shins as her heavy walking boots thumped heavily against the rough ground.

Rebecca was already feeling weary from the weeks of hiking and now the rucksack on her back, the camera and long long lens dangling in front of her and her satnav hooked to a belt loop of her cargo pants at her side, all started moving in different directions away from her body and smashing back into her again, accelerating their movement and feeling as if they were bruising her, each time one of her boots hit the hard ground. With all her, larger than she really wanted, major body parts joining in with the random directional movements of her equipment she realised that she must look frightening as she moved quicker and quicker, due to gravity, the downward gradient trying to force her into a forward roll.

She managed to shout through flapping cheeks. "Help me, help me," this time meaning it, and waited for a reaction. The man's reaction was not immediate. Fight or flight, he seemed to be thinking as he looked from the trench to his van and back, weighing up his options. Fight, was his panicked first decision but growling while throwing his spade roughly in Rebecca's direction was a pathetic act of frustration as it missed by about fifty metres and was always going to. He looked at the carpet again, apparently wondering if he could get it back into the van before the mad woman's arrival, and it was clearly time for Rebecca to help him with his choices as she wanted, above all else, for that carpet to be left where it was.

She did something she hated doing, had only done twice before in her life and something that was always a last resort. She struggled, while still running, to open a zipped pocket in the leg of her trousers, took out the small pistol, made sure it was not pointing anywhere near her body, flicked off the safety catch and 'Bang', the bullet flew high into the air and the bang echoed off surrounding hills. Rebecca stopped worrying about herself but,

12

instead, worried about where the bullet would eventually come down again to earth. Hopefully the shot would make the man choose immediate flight and Rebecca thought *damn Mr. Roberts, physics, for going on about ellipses and the fact that a bullet lands at the same speed it left the gun. Oh, where will it land? Not on top of someone's head, please.*

The man chose flight this time as he vaulted the gate to start the engine of his high topped van to drive away as quickly as he could. The sheep hardly moved at all, walking calmly away from Rebecca's path to find a slightly calmer pasture area. Chewing grass was their only concern in life.

She stopped as quickly as gravity would allow, put the safety back on, pocketed the gun and raised her camera up to her eye to take shots of the man's escape. Panting heavily, partly through sudden exertion and partly from the danger of the situation, she still had the composure to make sure that the little red focusing light in the middle of the lens missed the gate's timbers and focused on the van's registration plate as the van moved away.

I knocked him down to two hundred and fifty euros. She remembered out of the blue. *An hour of sex with an old man with a two foot long moustached who was very lonely except for his beloved goats was not the best offer I had that holiday but other scenarios had been almost as gross.*

The rest of the descent was an enforced walk on the flat of about twenty five yards as she tried to catch her breath and make a 999 call from her mobile at the same time. Her head slipped into another mode, a mode where she was super efficient and serious.

"Operation Country Hike, patch me through to Police Reserve Group HQ immediately please and if you don't know what that means then please ask your supervisor straight away."

The operator had obviously been briefed and didn't need to speak to her supervisor as Rebecca's call was instantly patched through to both PRG and the police at the same time and a voice at the other end said

"PRG. Your ID and position please"

"I'm 4063" replied Rebecca, still panting and trying to hold her mobile between her cheek and shoulder while fiddling with the Satnav that was still hooked on by the carabiner to the belt loop.

"And my co-ordinates are..."

She pressed three buttons on the satnav and the screen that had shown her bold blue line of travel across a map changed to a screen that gave her position in degrees, minutes and seconds both north and east and pin-pointed her position to within a couple of feet, which was great for someone who, unlike Rebecca, could understand the long and seemingly meaningless figures. Reading the numbers out slowly and without waiting for the next question she continued.

"Suspect, serial killer, I am one hundred percent sure, travelling from the position I just gave you in a westerly direction along a country lane in a white high-top van registration number..."

This time the satnav was dropped to fall back against her leg, finding the soreness from earlier and then dangled freely from the belt loop and the camera was up to her face and up near the shouldered phone as she flicked back through the shots on the rear camera screen. Finding one in clear focus, she then pressed on the magnifying glass button on the camera a couple of times to zoom in on the number plate and van make. She gave the operator the registration of the van in plane letters as she had never learnt that oscar-romeo language, she told the operator the van's colour again and the make and then;

"Two other things, an intended victim still, I believe, alive, not yet inspected by me and will require an ambulance. Secondly I will need an escape route out of here when the local plod arrives."

"Understood, please be aware you are connected also to local forces that are on their way to your position." was the reply, half in answer to her question and half to warn her not to use derogatory phrases like 'local plod'. Then the monotone, professional voice continued, repeating part of Rebecca's imparted information, and then, as if reading from a script which was, in Rebecca's mind, on a laminated card...

"Local police and ambulance have been listening to this call. Please wait where you are for them and don't touch anything or compromise the crime scene in any way. Now, if I could just take a few more details..."

Rebecca was careful to hang up before saying out loud to herself "Yeah, right, sorry love, signal just went" then, taking out her penknife, she started to cut away at the three lengths of sisal, looped and knotted around the carpet that was now, not only moving, but making muffled noises also.

She wasn't ready for the amount of purple, yellow and black bruising on the naked woman's shaking body but had to cut through tape binding her hands and feet before ripping, quickly, the tape from her mouth and remembering the pain of the waxing of her own moustache hair. The bruised lady exhaled a loud noise that tried to sum up her weeks of torture and rape and Rebecca pulled the woman into her chest to offer some form of comfort, some way to transfer some of that agony to herself as she repeated, what seemed like fifty times;

"It's all right, it's all over, and he's gone now and can't come back. I'm here and I won't let him anywhere near you."

When Rebecca cleared her head and could think again, and to cover herself from accusations about owning a gun for which she had no license, she added "He fired a shot at me but he's gone now and the gun with him." This would hopefully plant into the mind of 'bruised lady' a thought that she would probably mention as one of her own in her statement, saying that the man fired a shot at her rescuer, as if she had seen the action herself through the rolled up carpet. Internally, Rebecca was repeating, for her own benefit, a chant, a mantra that went "Not all men are bastards, some are, but not all, please God, not all men are bastards."

'Bruised lady' sobbed constantly, trying to get words out but failing and Rebecca knew that she couldn't let go of her completely so was forced to, one handed, remove her rucksack, open the top flap and pull out a bath- towel gently placing it around the woman for the sake of both her modesty and to try and stop her shivering, although it was obvious that the shivering was not from cold weather. She purposely didn't ask the woman her name as that would then have made things too personal and could affect Rebecca's state of mind in the future. She would remain as 'bruised lady' until the trial, in which Rebecca would hopefully, not for the first time, appear not in person but in a video link. Things had moved so quickly that it wasn't until much later that day that it really hit home to Rebecca what the horror of this situation really was. The realisation that what she had stopped was to have been a live burial. The wondering also of what would have happened if she had stopped to take even more blue-tit photos.

Two local police officers arrived on the scene, one male one female, in a local police car that looked as if it had been passed down from force to smaller force, and eventually down to their village station. An overweight male constable appeared to Rebecca to be walking for the first time in weeks and looked alien away from his car. His demure, much younger, female partner approached with him, but not before a helicopter had passed over a couple of times, moving, eventually, in the direction that Rebecca has reported. A sobbing 'Bruised lady' was forcefully prised away from the safety of Rebecca's arms and into the hands of the female officer who led her to the police car and the stone faced male officer had clearly been told not to interview Rebecca but looked at her intently as she had now dramatically pulled up her snood from around her neck; the snood that apparently had twenty five different positions and different uses but Rebecca could only work out three. She walked towards the male officer looking like a bandit from an early cowboy film, the snood covering her from her neck up to just below her eyes that, she now regretted, bore no makeup. A famous photo of a refugee woman, face covered apart from intense, penetrating eyes came to her mind and quickly flitted away on imagining how she now actually looked to the officer. She spoke firmly as if she was his superior and may even have attempted enlarging her eyes.

"You are now witnessing me taking the memory card from my camera and you need to make a note of the time please. That would be in your notebook, yeah."

She smiled under the snood as he scrambled for his book and picked the pen up from the floor. She had formed the ground rules, she was dictating what happened.

"The times on the actual shots will be imbedded on the photos themselves, not on the picture but within the background file information. The memory card needs to go into an evidence bag and sealed to show a clear path of evidence and no tampering of the digital shots. This is the knife with which I cut the sisal that was around that carpet lying over there, the carpet that the woman was wrapped up in and this is the tape that was around her mouth so more evidence bags needed please and note the penknife has my finger prints all over it, the tape may have the suspect's prints, I only touched two corners. There will be cross contamination between me and the victim; my DNA and fingerprints file will be forwarded to your superiors and to forensic, with a number and not my name attached to it within the next couple of days, this is standard routine. The towel she has around her was mine and not the suspects. Do you have all that?"

He didn't, he was still writing so Rebecca purposely continued.

"Hopefully you have some crime scene tape to place around the area and a method of stopping passers-by from stopping for a break and to take holiday pictures?"

The officer still looked vacant and she thought about mentioning the blue tit photos on the memory card, decided against but smiled, under her snood, noting that the officer was dressed in a blue uniform.

"Nobody, by the way, has touched the spade that's up the hill, since the suspect threw it."

Rebecca had received minimal training for the civilian job she was doing but had been told, most emphatically, that she had not joined the intelligence service or anything vaguely similar; that she would be protected, if needed, by the police in the UK but not abroad where she would be on her own and, if caught abroad, could be accused of spying. Lastly, she had been told that if she acted in a superior manner with the local police in the UK, who would have been fore-warned not to interview her, then she would be assumed to be Special Forces and it would not be lying, or perverting the course of justice, to let people think whatever they wanted to think without them knowing the actual truth. Also, she enjoyed talking down to a male copper; it gave her the upper hand, the power and control that she thrived on.

The officer did not answer her but she could hear the cogs in his brain clunking over with *Bloody trying to teach me my job* type thoughts and at that moment her phone rang giving her an excuse to turn her back on him, end the conversation with the officer on her terms and walk away back up the hill a few paces, looking and feeling superior and in charge of the situation having delegated the mundane tasks to him. The phone showed a picture of her boss and the name she had given him on her phone not to reveal his true identity 'Geordie' being the not so subtle name under the photo. Not wishing to give any hint of either her working background or

Geordie's identity she just answered the phone with a muffled "Hi" through the snood.

"We've only gone and bloody caught him." The excited voice on the other end said without introduction.

"Thanks to you, that woman with you isn't victim number seven and there will be no number eight – you have photos putting him at the scene, right?" Geordie's voice sounded hopeful.

Rebecca explained in minimalist phrases what was on the one memory card that was now with the local police, withholding for the time being the information that her camera had dual memory card slots and that she had an exact copy for Geordie when she saw him, which would be after she had copied the photos to the hard drive of her laptop without anyone knowing. Then she asked Geordie where and how the suspect had been caught after briefly describing the shots of the scene and of the number plate.

"It was easy. The plate you gave us, not false, so registered of course at the DVLA, belongs to the suspect who lives at a local residential caravan park and when we got there he was sat in his caravan pretending to have been there all day but with a red hot van engine outside and we had film from the copter of him pulling up at the site. Forensic are taking his van away on a low loader and crawling all over the caravan and if there's no trace of the woman or the carpet inside the back of his van I'll eat my hat. People on the site have told us that the guy has a yard in town where he keeps his stuff for his plumbing business so forensic will be following police there, afterwards. I was told you rang the reg plate through but, until you just said, I had no idea you had photos of it and him with the spade. He won't stand a chance in court."

Rebecca managed to contain her pride and excitement verbally and Geordie could not see her beaming smug smile.

"Will you be able to tell me what you find at his yard Geordie, especially if there's another woman captive there and also, can you get me out of here mate?"

But Geordie had everything already planned.

"The police chopper you've probably seen flying about is coming back for you." Geordie answered, "There's big money in this for you Rebecca and this time it will be in sterling so you'll be able to spend it a bit easier than after your normal European drug busts. I'm arranging the various rewards that have been placed to be paid in cash but will decline the newspaper rewards, on your behalf, as they're attached to exclusive interviews and photos, and we don't want that do we, for the sake of this victim and her dead mates. A mis-trial now would be a tragedy."

That was a statement and not a question, thought Rebecca so she didn't answer but concentrated on the two words "this victim." Yes she had saved the life of 'bruised lady' but she was still, very much, the victim and would be for the rest of her life. The chopper arrived, breaking her train of thought and almost made a landing but had to hover a foot above the sloping ground. Rebecca shouted her goodbye into the phone to Geordie not being able to hear any reply and threw her rucksack into the cockpit before climbing in, strapping herself in tightly and being handed a helmet with a radio link to the pilot. The pilot was already talking, presumably to air traffic control, in terms that went over Rebecca's head but she did hear him mention Penzance. He then flicked a switch and talked directly, to Rebecca through their head sets.

"I've been told not to ask any questions and with that mask covering your face I'm guessing you're intelligence or something?"

"That was a question" was Rebecca's reply and the rest of the flight was carried out in an awkward silence. Rebecca found herself in the weird situation of trying to come down off the adrenaline buzz of her day, trying not to think too much about what would have happened to 'Bruised lady' if she had spent more time sat in the wood and, at the same time, she was thoroughly enjoying the spectacular views from this, her first ever helicopter ride. She spent the journey trying to work out where she was, the names of places she could see below her and was thrilled at how it all looked like one of her colourful maps down there below her, but also trying to act uninterested in front of the pilot as if she had done this many times. Just before landing the pilot revealed to her that she was being dropped off at the old Penzance helipad and he hoped that it was convenient for her. It was extremely convenient because she had shopping to do in the local supermarket across the road from the helipad, using the list she'd made two nights before in her tent, her fridge being intentionally emptied before her hiking trip. She kept that to herself and just nodded to the pilot and wondered how easy it would be to transform from hero to domesticated shopping woman.

Hello checkout woman, I just caught the raping murderer, by the way, the one that you've read about in the papers and worry about when you go out at night.

Thank you madam, do you have a loyalty card?

The rest of the day was a blur in Rebecca's later, short and long term memory as she had tried to block out of her mind the horrific part of the day and at the same time she felt guilty, knowing that 'bruised lady' had much more to try and deal with and probably never would be able to block things out. In reality, only partly later remembered by Rebecca, she had walked away from the helicopter, doing the 'crouching while running' thing even though her height was nowhere near the helicopter blade height - but it felt like the thing to do as she had seen it done on the telly and in films. She had then crossed the main road to the local supermarket removing the snood from her face as if had been there as a defence against the dust thrown up by the helicopter. She quietly did some food shopping with all the 'ordinary folk' wondering if her trouser bum was still wet or stained and if stained hopefully not in a horrible colour *isn't the tannin colour from oak leaves a sort of poo colour?* And then took a taxi to a car park that was near to her four storey home in St. Ives, walking the last hundred yards as she always did but this time weighed down by a rucksack and four carrier bags. In the taxi she had contemplated how well the day had gone, how efficient she had been, how good she was at her job and the contrast between that and her private life where she was a completely unorganised, very lonely, relationship failure. It seemed that life had dealt her a hand of cards that could only be played as a do-gooder, loner, with a need for power and a hater of those that had power over her, especially if they happened to have male gender.

She climbed the stairs of her home, passed the exit off the stairs to her living room and carried on up to her kitchen area. She threw her rucksack, camera and satnav into a corner, emptied the carrier bags into the fridge and cupboards and undressed in the corridor. Moving next door to the bathroom she showered and, towel-wrapped she climbed another flight to the bedroom area and dressed to go out. She put on tight but real denim jeans (jeggins were a young woman's cheat and looked like a cheat) that took an age to get on while laying on her back on her bed, but they felt a million miles away from loose cargo trousers with a wet stain on the bum and added to the jeans a white shirt-blouse, crisp and clean but see-through enough to show off the lacy bra and with a calculated number of buttons left undone. The heels she chose because of their complete incompatibility with the cobbled streets around her home and the fact that they were the complete opposite of hiking boots. She added a bullet to the empty slot in the chamber of her gun, placed the gun in her safe, went out to the nearest local pub and got thoroughly legless, on her own with nobody to talk to and nobody that she particularly wanted to talk to and, let's face it, what conversation could she have? "Hi, thingy, what did you do today?" She was, of course, completely unaware and uncaring about the vulnerable state she was getting herself into after every vodka and orange taken.

Chapter 2

The hot summer sun streamed into the third floor bedroom of Rebecca's home, slowly tracking across the room, illuminating tiny, floating, dust particles until it eventually reached the bed and warmed the outers of her closed eyes. The sun's intensity and the stove simmering effect that it caused made swirling patterns in her eyes, bubbles of yellow swam around on a red background and nauseated her. Inevitably, this would force a full waking into reality from her alcohol induced sleep as she lay on her side with a sweaty face stuck to the pillow, almost aware that she had been snoring and dribbling. She was being annoyed by the sun's direct rays but was incapable of moving her head away from them or turning over. Occasionally, shadows crossed her face, darkening the visible red in her eyes and, for Rebecca, they were reassuring shadows known to be made by gulls as they darted from side to side of their open stage which was the large, glazed, inward opening doors with Juliet balcony. It was mid-morning in her vague way of judging time by the suns position and, as she drifted into consciousness, she could feel tight clothing wrapped around her and could feel the sweat between the clothing and her body; the smell of alcohol and artificial orange was putrid.

I managed to keep my clothes on last night but I'm pretty sure I've offended someone or done something really embarrassing.

This was a thought, not mumbled speech as Rebecca, was unable to move her mouth or feel her tongue.

She was in her bed that faced the Juliet balcony, high above the rest of the world. The bed had a fantastically beautiful view across the harbour and across the bay to Hayle, but today the view would mean nothing to her and would be boringly taken for granted. She had designed each floor of the building, selfishly affording the best view to her lonesome self and her bed on the very top floor rather than keep the top storey living room that she had found when she'd bought the place, but it was a view that would be ignored now as she was stirring from an uncomfortable sleep that had taken place with no recollection of arriving at either the bed, or her home. Eyes still tightly shut in fear, tongue dry and slowly, one millimetre at a time, peeling from the roof of her foul-tasting mouth, her most immediate thoughts centred on survival based on thirst, the dire need for a pee, the fear of a raging headache if she were to move her head and whether all of these feelings could please go away if she could just be allowed to lapse back into sleep for a tiny, little bit longer.

The local gull's noise that she had slept through today was usually Rebecca's alarm clock and was

now being tuned into focus within her shrivelled
brain. The gulls, with their yelping, laughing and
wailing, usually gave her reassurance, letting her
know which of her three homes she was in while
she drifted out of sleep, there being very few gulls
on Greek islands, for some reason, and fewer still
at her inland French vineyard home. She raised
her head slowly from the pillows to avoid the
expected vodka dizziness and the cloth of the
pillow eventually released the skin of her cheek.
Robot like, she staggered the few steps to her en-
suite loo while attempting to move her tongue in
an effort to form saliva and trying not to burp, just
in case. Empty bladdered and partially refilled with
three week old, not-so-fizzy but who cares, bottled
water that she'd found beside the bed, she
staggered to the open glass doors and gripped
tightly onto the top of the glazed balcony screen
for her first glimpse of what was going on in the
world and to get air into her lungs that didn't have
a smell that made her feel nauseous. Looking
down she felt dizzy due to the height and her
hangover so immediately threw back her head
wildly and looked up towards the gulls.

These gulls were normally fun to watch. It was
the month of June, building to the very height of
the tourist season. The town gull numbers were
increasing every day as the tourist numbers
increased. Tourists were third in the gull food
production line behind fishing boats and council

rubbish tips but still, the tourists did offer a healthy bonus. The local council had erected small yellow signs stating that the gulls shouldn't be fed but the gulls didn't read the signs so new signs were added, aimed this time at the tourists, the signs proclaiming 'ice cream and chip thieves operate in this area.' The gulls still readily swooped out of the sky, returning vertically with a half pasty or a beak full of chips, leaving behind a crying child or, as once witnessed from this very spot, an ice cream stolen from a screaming group of hysterical, young, teenage, girls half scared and half thankful for the attention of centre stage; each screaming girl looking in all directions hoping for an audience. Those victims of the gulls, still left with half a meal, often failed to realise that the beak that had entered their food was, earlier that day, probably scavenging in the local rubbish tip and the eater would carry on munching through the germs, unable to admit the loss of the whole meal. It was usually also a great balcony for looking down at the world, seeing the different characters of the tourists of many nations. It was from this balcony, last summer, that Rebecca had breathed in deeply the fresh air, reaching her lungs directly from the Atlantic Ocean and then, looked down and saw a family, their faces hidden behind surgical face masks but still discernible as being Japanese and believing, presumably, that they were walking through the petrol fumed atmosphere of a large city, like Tokyo.

Rebecca closed the doors to the world to shut out the noise and the warm air and pushed her fingers through her hair, hoping for some sort of miracle that would make her look and feel half decent. Knowing that the miracle hadn't happened she turned back towards her bed expecting to get more sleep but looked up and jumped with shock, breathed in rapidly and clutched at where she thought her heart probably was, at the same time shouting at the bloke standing in the doorway.

"Kitto, what the hell are you doing wandering around my flat?"

Kitto looked hurt at first but then managed his usual huge, toothy, friendly smile as he realised that his friend had no recollection of last night.

"Heard you moving about, thought I'd catch you before you started to get changed or something. Embarrassing that would be. I've been sleeping downstairs above the shop, on your settee. Brought you home last night, someone had to; worried you could choke on your sick the state you were in."

Kitto turned as if to leave and let Rebecca contemplate his words and wonder if anything had happened between them but he turned just his head back again to see Rebecca's face still in shock and puzzlement and he wondered if she was clutching her heart or hiding her cleavage from him.

He said his three beat poem casually and quietly;

"Coffee, white, no sugar"

It was a statement rather than a question and he turned again to go downstairs, confident that as he had been in an alcoholic state so many times himself, that he knew what Rebecca was probably going through, and, more importantly, how he could help what he regarded as his friend. Rebecca eventually followed like a lost sheep and was trying to walk without moving her head too much and still doing the 'miracle with the fingers through the hair' thing and wondering where the nearest mirror was and then wondering whether looking into it would make her feel even worse.

Where are those bloody face-covering sunglasses when you need them?

She was incapable of any constructive feelings but felt a strange invasion of her privacy. She regarded her home as her playroom from childhood, where her academic parents had filled their only child's life with dolls and stuffed playmates, out of the way, not untidying the house for when guests came, lonely, in her own world of play.

Rebecca followed Kitto down the stairs from her en-suited sleeping area to the kitchen and bathroom level where they both left the staircase before it descended down another flight to the living room and then down again to the front door next to the shop that Rebecca rented out to someone who knew what they were doing with a shop, as she would have had no idea.

"Look Kitto, thanks for getting me home but I still don't understand..."

"Ranting you were." The word seemed to sum it all up for Kitto.

"Pardon?" Rebecca knew she'd been drunk but that word was not her. Surely not.

Kitto made the coffee as if it was his own flat. He knew where everything was kept and looked quite at home, quite domesticated and probably enjoying the responsibility of looking after her. Rebecca sat at the pine kitchen table, on a pine bench facing Kitto and his coffee making, as if she was a guest in her own flat. Looking down at the ground, she realised how dated the floor covering was under her bare feet, how dated the mock pine furniture had become and how the room had been neglected. It was not the room of someone who liked being in a kitchen, who enjoyed cooking. It felt like a holiday-let made up from the owners old furniture. Kitto, meanwhile, boiled the kettle with his back to her to spare her blushes while he answered her non understanding of the word ranting.

"Don't know where you'd been drinking earlier but when I came across you, you were in the

Ketch Inn, luckily in one of those booths so not everyone could hear you ranting"

There's that word again, ranting thought Rebecca wondering why it sounded so sinister, so much like there was going to be embarrassment attached to it.

"Packed it was cos it was meat raffle night. Could see you were off your head and staggering so kept a watchful eye on you. Then saw you get refused a vodka orange at the bar, cos you were so far gone, so I came over to the bar to help out, mediate, sort of thing. You'd got nasty by the time I got over to you, demanding from the barmaid two steaks, even though she'd told you chef had gone home. Said you wanted the free bottle of red wine that comes with the steaks, would pay for the steaks and they could owe you the meals when chef came back next day. Made Mike smile, he was behind barmaid in case of trouble. You points then to the basket of raw meat won by someone in the raffle, then to a painting for sale on the wall showing the back of a nude woman and you starts ranting some feminist things and shouted to a group of women there in the pub to beware of their blokes and told them they might have been lumps of fresh meat if it weren't for you. Then you got angry cos a few people were laughing at you so I calmed you and helped you out, nodding to Mike that I'd get you out before he threw you out. Practically carried you home after the fresh air

36

knocked you out. Found your key in your back pocket, could see keys impression, jeans being that tight, not that I'd been looking, you understand, got you to top floor over my shoulder without you being sick down my back luckily. Thought for a while about getting you undressed for bed, decided I liked my lovers to be at least semi-conscious, thank you very much, so shoved you on your bed, prised your dagger like shoes off, threw sheet over you and came downstairs to settee so I could hopefully hear if you started chucking up. Bout sums things up really."

Kitto turned from the worktop to the table, a mug of steaming coffee in each hand to see Rebecca, head bowed down supported by her hands, embarrassed and thinking she needed something a bit more substantial than the mug of instant placed in front of her. As more and more café cum coffee shops had arrived in St. Ives, competition meant that the coffee price had gone down dramatically to the point that if Kitto wasn't there then she would have gone out to get a very large take-away cappuccino with an extra shot for a couple of quid. But she knew that Kitto was enjoying the intimacy of the two of them being in the same room as much as she was forced into the role of feeble female incapable of looking after herself and needing a man to sort her out. She couldn't quite work out however what the attraction was as she was sure that if she had been

Kitto then she would be running away from this mess of sweat, smell and smudged makeup.

All the time Kitto had been talking, Rebecca's mind had been racing, questions forming about the night that was a blank and would forever be an empty file in the hard drive of her memory bank. If Kitto had 'Practically carried her home' and then carried her upstairs over his shoulder then where did that swap happen and how many people that she knew saw it, and did she really care? When she was over the mighty shoulders of Kitto, where had his supporting hands been? How long had it taken Kitto to get the key out of her back pocket and how much had he enjoyed himself doing it? None of this she spoke, of course, politely croaking out.

"Thanks Kitto, you're a pal. Sounds like I could have ended up in the gutter last night. I don't remember anything. I'm embarrassed enough now so big thanks for leaving the clothes on, yeah"

They both smiled. There was an unspoken agreement between them and it was taken for granted that Kitto had always fancied Rebecca, may even have been in love with her and would do anything for her but knew from casual conversations that they had shared that she had been badly hurt a number of times and was anti-bloke and anti-settling down at that moment so he made no move and Rebecca did nothing to encourage him.

Taking sips of coffee and following the hot
liquid's path down the left half of her throat, her
head was full of gratitude for Kitto's friendship and
she was also wondering when the right hand side
of her throat would wake up. She wasn't exactly
thinking straight so it was a few days after this
episode, when Rebecca looked back on it, that she
realised the possible, tragic, irony of the situation if
it had happened differently and some other bloke
other than Kitto had carried her up her stairs. For
Rebecca to capture a serial rapist who killed his
victims, provide the evidence that would probably
send him down, go out to celebrate with vodka
and get in a state, be carried upstairs by someone
she may not have known and certainly wouldn't
remember, not in any way be able to give consent
to and to therefore be raped in her own bed. It
would have been ironic indeed, frightening really,
a reason to cut down on alcohol intake, hate men
even more and to be even more grateful to Kitto –
who was, of course, confusingly, a man.

She was recovering slowly. Kitto had found
some paracetamol for her in the bathroom
cabinet, and provided another mug of coffee
which she tried to add to her stomach contents as
she looked across the table at him. He was still
dressed in his going out clothes. He had on a tidy
tee shirt but they always looked too small on him
due to his very muscular physique. Rebecca had
known friends and boyfriends who had invested

huge amounts of money and time in the gym, failing to look anything like that. Rebecca would never be in charge of his wardrobe but, if she was...

A memory came to her as if her brain had found first gear. Kitto had once, only once (her choice), taken her out on his boat and sent out a hand-line for her with six mackerel feathers and a large lead weight and Rebecca had worried about how she was going to get the heavy weight back to the boat, never mind any fish. She caught three mackerel at the same time and watched Kitto laugh uncontrollably as she struggled for ages to pull them in, with her thankfully gloved, hands. Sweating and sitting at the front of the boat with tired arm muscles she had then been treated to a display proudly given by Kitto as he let out what seemed to be hundreds of hooks and pulled it all back in with alternate hands, the biceps and triceps of each arm on much intended show to her. It was a sight that had started to slightly excite her until he started to flick each mackerel off the hook and into the bottom of the boat near her feet, the feet that she had to bring up close to her chest to avoid the flapping fish. But she never forgot Kitto's pride or his physique or, unfortunately, the flapping, dying fish or her screams as if she were a little girl.

She snapped back into the present where coffee was being drunk in silence until it was Kitto's turn to look and sound embarrassed as he wondered where Rebecca's head had been while he had been talking and knowingly ignored.

"Don't know where you've been these last few weeks, missed you though, can't stop here chopsing though 'cos tide don't wait for man, as they say and I'm fishing low tide today hoping mackerel will shoal tight before coming back in to eat the sandeel, and I need to get the boat ready and out of harbour while there's still water under it. You're okay now I reckon. Thanks for the coffee and settee. You need a longer one by the way; my calves are aching from hanging over the arm."

And with that Kitto was off down the stairs with Rebecca shouting her thanks after him, smiling and wondering where her key was, how quickly she could shower last night off and how to make the house cool enough for sleep.

Shuffling slowly back upstairs, mug still in her hand, Rebecca knew that although all the heat in her chimney shaped house rose up to her bedroom, it was there that the air conditioning unit was mounted in the ceiling and there that she could flop back onto her bed to sleep in the cool. She turned towards the air conditioner control box with all its mysterious and magic symbols and pressed the only button she understood, the on-off button, and the thing fired up allowing her to lay on her bed still fully dressed. Without sleeping she growled at the sound the unit made as if it was the tenth thing that had gone wrong that day.

From above the ceiling she heard an annoying knocking noise and, her body and mind still not quite coordinating, she thought about whether she could fix the metronomic clacking. It had started to annoy her even before she went away, trekking the countryside, weeks earlier. Whether she would have to get someone in to look at the air con and whether, if she had turned it on earlier, she could have asked Kitto to take a look at it were all now historical thoughts and both involved a total reliance on gallant men helping a damsel in distress. Without really thinking about it, she found herself climbing the ladder that was kept permanently sloping upward from the top of her staircase, to the ceiling hatch that was at the same angle as her roof slope. Then, Rebecca and her tight jeans went bum-first through the roof's skylight, breach-birthed into the hot, but clean air. Scampering, barefoot, down the washed out light-blue roof slates, carefully avoiding any damage to the natural covering of fluorescent orange lichen, she reached the central flat-roof area, with four Cornish-slate pitched roofs surrounding it, only one of which had been cemented over in traditional Cornish repair-it fashion. Then she sat for a moment to catch her breath. This was where the other end of the air conditioning unit sat, the big box with the cooling fan, hidden away from ground floor view and in a place where nobody else had ever been invited. This was Rebecca's special place.

She often laid down on this warm, black, flat-roof sunbathing naked with no chance of being overlooked by anyone and removing all her white bits, but this time she was in the sweaty, once white, shirt, tight jeans and red-mark-making underwear that she had slept in and now she was trying to work out the logic behind what was facing her. In some sort of demonic, voodoo, puppet enactment, a messenger had flown in to keep her awake, to try to force her from staying in her home being unsocial. A seagull's bleached white skeleton of head and cannibalised body along with still pink legs and partly feathered wings, was tapping its beak continuously against the side of the air conditioning fan casing, tapping out the beat to a tune that only the skeleton itself could hear and leaving scratch marks with its beak on the casing's paintwork.

She was more curious than troubled and stared questionably at the skeleton, hating the idea of not being able to work the thing out and wondering briefly if she was still asleep and that Kitto and the seagull skeleton were part of a weird dream. Then she saw the fishing line. The gull, it appeared, had taken a holidaymaker's fishing bait, complete with hook, which she now noticed was piercing the gull's cheek. The silvered hook, that had partly rusted and also a fair length of line had travelled with the gull for, who knew how long, until finally and fatally, the loose end of the line, blowing in the wind, had found the revolving cooling fan of the air conditioning unit. Wrapping the line around the central pulley, the fan had slowly pulled the gull into the casing and kept it there denying it of its sustenance and its freedom.

When she grabbed the skeleton head with two hands and pulled, the line snapped in a place where it had previously worn and the tapping sound stopped leaving only the muffled sound of the invisible streets below, not consciously heard until that moment. Rebecca quickly dropped the now loose bones into a small pile, vowing to clear them up later and to wash her hands even before showering and then, using her removed sweaty shirt as a very poor pillow, keeping everything else on but unbuttoned and unhooked, she closed her eyes to the sun for a supposed couple of minutes. She thought of Kitto, how good a friend he was, how much he cared for her, how he appeared to care more for her than he did for himself, and how she liked him, maybe even loved him, but not in that sort of way. As she drifted off into sleep she was wondering about all the blokes that she had had 'that feeling' for and who had later turned out to be pigs. Perhaps there was, after all, a case for the arranged marriage scenario of marrying your bloke and then slowly coming to love him.

Waking she heard the stupid notes from her mobile that meant she had a text. Her eyes focussed, eventually, on the phone screen. She shielded the screen from the strong sun and noticed, from the clock on the screen that she had been asleep for over an hour and, she smiled when she realised the text was from Geordie and was one of his cryptic messages that unnecessarily meant that nobody but Rebecca could understand the meaning, as if it mattered somehow.

"Tomorrow. Wed. Usual London park café. 10am???"

She had the local train ticket-office in her contact list on her phone as she had used it a number of times and preferred speaking to someone rather than booking a train on-line. She had always found that explaining your needs to a human that was conversant with time tables and could do the work for you was better than logical computer suggestions with fifteen different options. Within minutes she had chatted with the woman at the other end of the line, explained that she wanted shopping time after her meeting and that she didn't like getting up early in the morning (you can't tell that to a computer) and, together, they booked her into a private sleeper compartment on the, little known, sleeper train that left St. Ives at 9.45 that night, and they (shall WE do that then?) also booked the return journey starting at 10 pm the following night from

Paddington. The woman on the other end of the line appeared excited as if they were travelling together and, Rebecca worked out, the extra cost of these sleeper journeys was easily more economical than staying in a London hotel for a night at her own cost and it would give her time to get sober and make herself human again. Her route-march would be; travel while sleeping overnight tonight, breakfast near the station, meet Geordie, shop in London in the afternoon, evening meal in the Greek restaurant where she had previously heard plotting and possible illegal activity but all in Greek and then sleeper back to St. Ives to arrive around seven the next morning, refreshed and ready to go and not feeling like she did at the moment. As usual, to avoid any traceable bank transactions, she paid for her train tickets using her store credit card that she would pay off, in store, in London, with cash of which she had plenty and the promise of a lot more from Geordie. A good night's sleep on the train and she would arrive at Paddington at 5.30 in the morning and could decide between then and 7.00 am when to leave the train, go for a nice breakfast and then walk to the stated park café for her meeting. There was nothing left for her to do for the rest of the day other than showering, and putting on crisp, clean, very loose clothing.

She typed into the return text box
"Yeah, ok"

Send, whoosh.

Send now to Kitto

"Away two days, thanks again friend, speak when I get back, Bec x (delete x)"

Send, whoosh.

Chapter 3

The journey to London had started just before dusk and as she walked the familiar route to the local train station at the edge of St. Ives she was in contemplative mood. She could never decide whether it was a good thing or a bad thing to leave her adopted town and so she stopped by the fresh-water stream that emptied onto the beach as if she was going to lean on the railings and decide. The gulls were calmer here, no squabbling for food, a never ending supply of drinking water for all meant that there was no need for barking cries, no hierarchy among the drinking gulls, no survival of the fittest. She had wondered, at one time, why they drank as they did and she had looked it up in the library before the internet search revolution. The noisy beggars had tongues but couldn't lap, so filled their lower beaks with water and then threw their heads back to get the water down their throats. As she watched them it reminded her of drinking shots which made her think of vodka and orange which made her feel sick and so she threw her day-sack back onto one shoulder and walked on towards the station trying to get shot drinking out of her head, trying not to burp up a taste of orange.

She loved the town, and her building, but there was something very insular about living there, as if it was a very small island where, if you weren't secretive or secluded like her, then everyone would know your business and there was a need to get off the island now and again, or go mad. In the cold and the rain of winter, the slate and granite that made up the town was dark and drab and the town became as-one with the rocky outcrops, but in the summer, the contrast between the drab browns of the granite and the bright sun shining off the azure coloured sea was too much of a contrast for the eyes to take. It was a very English scenario that had been worked out and conquered by the Greeks a long time ago by a cunning use of colour on their buildings.

She had a deep regret that there were fewer Cornish people in the town now and felt guilty that she was part of that problem, being an incomer. As a Welsh speaker who had later learnt English at the age of five, she had thought a couple of times about learning Cornish but had not joined a class, her excuse being that hundreds of words in Cornish were very similar, but not quite the same as in Welsh and she would get confused between the two languages. It was bad enough that she already got confused between the little French and Greek that she had when visiting France or Greece. She was forever using Greek words in France, for instance and wondering why the locals couldn't understand her. From Wales to Cornwall, she thought, it was the same old story. When the local industry, in this case the large-scale fishing industry of Cornwall, started to decline, some locals whose families had lived and fished there for generations, turned to tourism as a means of income. Tourism took over as the main industry but it took all day for holiday makers to get to St. Ives and the other Cornish tourist towns, through narrow roads and towns without bypasses. Motorways and dual carriageways were built to get the tourists there quicker and easier and this cut the travel time down, from a day, to a few hours. Visitors on holiday liked the area, moved in just like Rebecca had, house prices went up, locals moved out and now practically every building in St. Ives was a shop, a café, a restaurant, a gallery, a guest house or a holiday let.

Rebecca had only one real person that she could speak to in St. Ives, Kitto, and then not in much depth, passing news perhaps, each of them afraid of the commitment to a solid friendship, to knowing too much about each other. They had revealed to each other, over the years, little snippets of their lives but only in comparison with the trivia they were discussing and so, for instance, when Shaun had been caught by his wife, in bed with Julia who made sure that everyone knew, Rebecca had shared how she had caught out others, how she had been hurt, how she was off relationships, and without actually saying it - how Kitto should please keep a friendly distance. There were a lot of people that she recognised and said hello to but nobody else that she could call a real friend, just people who passed in the street, quickly, as if they had somewhere important to go by a certain time and shouted something like "Hi love, how are you" not able to call her by name but recognising her face from a shop or a pub. No friends now, through choice, back in South Wales or at her small farmhouse and vineyard in France and only one friend, a woman who cleaned for her, at her Greek island home but she hadn't spoken to her for a year, or was it longer? Her life was on auto-pilot and she suddenly snapped out of her thoughts having arrived at the station. The guard was kindly finding her compartment for her.

As her train moved off she lay on her back on the bed of her personal single sleeper compartment, occasionally looking at the door handle to assure herself that the door was locked as she listened to the clickety clack of the wheels in the gaps between rails and her mind wandered to how on earth she got to be the person she was now.

...and it was great that mam and dad let me stay on in the bungalow in Cardiff when they moved to teach at university in North Wales. That allowed me to keep my job in day care of young adults with learning difficulties as well as allowing me to keep my freedom - the bungalow, the place where everyone congregated nightly away from their

parents, great at first, party time, then boring, then
feeling used, realising that it was the bungalow that
was popular, not me, finding it occupied even if I
wasn't there, the decision to get out, the camping
trip with the gang of eight to Llyn Brianne in Mid-
Wales, my final decision to stay on in camp when
everyone went back home, sat there wondering
where they would all go without access to the
bungalow...the poem I wrote in my tent listening to
the rain on the canvas...

From Teenage kicks and twenties lows I walked.
Alone,   from tented camp and climbed the
mountain high.   Above you
all to watch the hawks hold hands,   And
plummet down towards your ennui.

I shout to warn the boulder's left my hands,
From one mile up I still can smell your fear.
Run wild you skittles now personified,
In different worlds, and ever more to be.

At last, to Dinas' ancient oaks I spoke
Though pied flycatcher's somersaults distract
I told them of the change in me. They said
You know, it soon will be the time to leave.

Your last night there, I shared a line of trees
On river's bank I was a willow tree
And when the bats at last came out to feed

They flew my face to wonder at this drunk.
I've lost myself in nature not with man
Please, drive off in the morning everyone.

Like the fake timber sign in Debbie's kitchen
"If friends were flowers, I'd pick you" and my first
thought being that a week after flower picking,
comes the death of the flower,.....selling the
bungalow, buying a terraced valleys house,
investing a huge amount of money– the difference
in city and village house prices... realising nobody
from the old gang was contacting me, meeting the
new women, especially bossy Linda, her actually
telling me, not asking me, that we were going on
holiday to the Canaries, the holiday that changed
my life...

Rebecca had gone through a period in her life
where everything was on an even keel with no ups
and downs, aka boring. Something like Linda
telling her that they were going on holiday
together, rather than asking her, would normally
have annoyed her controlling mind, but something
inside her told her to go with the flow, accept
being bossed and see where it took her. It took
her, initially, to four pre-holiday weeks of fake
smiles, trying to be enthusiastic about Linda's
constant talking about makeup, hair and what
clothes to wear on each of the fourteen nights of
the holiday. At one point Rebecca suspected that

the whole point of the holiday and the contents of their suitcases was to get Linda permanently fixed up with a bloke. Rebecca saw it more as a chance to relax in the sun, maybe see some sights, or maybe she was making one huge mistake.

The first week of the holiday had been a non-compromising normal girls holiday of drinking at night and into early morning, minimal sleep, waking to go to the beach to sleep some more in the sun, an early evening of listening to Linda discussing what she would wear that night, and repeat...

The pace of the holiday was beginning to get to them both and they agreed to have an easy night but not too easy, still going to a club but drinking less and that was the night where they met the couple who were at least twice their age but nice to talk to and keeping the evening calm and relaxed and mature. They both enjoyed the older couple's company and chatted for about an hour before world war three broke out.

Men, and women, hooded and dressed all in black from head to foot appeared from everywhere, in Rebecca's later incorrect and exaggerated memory they even abseiled down ropes from the ceiling like in a Bond movie. It soon became apparent that they were all heavily armed and the club was either being robbed by ninjas or raided by the police. Rebecca was standing at a small bar in the corner of the room chatting to her new older friend, him talking through his untrimmed moustache that filtered out the head of his beer, making you stare at the froth, while Linda was sat nearby with his wife. The music was cut, the house lights went up and megaphones cut through the noise and screams.

"Lie down, on the ground, now, face down, everyone" came the orders from all those in black to everyone else, first in English and then what was presumably Spanish, and nearly everyone did lie down.

"Not you" said Rebecca's new friend with the moustache. I know you're clean.

The situation hit Rebecca head on, it was a drugs raid and her new friend was part of the police side of things. Then she heard Linda's excited, high pitched, valleys accented voice...

"In this dress, you want me to lie down on your stinking, beer-stained floor in this dress, have you any idea how much I paid for this dress?"

Moustache spoke softly to Rebecca "Tell her."

"Linda, get down or get hurt, we'll get it dry cleaned" and Linda hit the floor just before a rifle butt could push her in that direction.

"I am in charge of this operation but like to take a back seat" moustache boasted with some pride as men like to do when talking about their authority. Rebecca, for some reason, thought that if 'moustache' had been a peacock then his tail would be fanned out now.

"I guess you're looking for the tall guy in the pink shirt then and also green jumper, lying next to him, his runner" Rebecca answered, almost nonchalantly with equal, but hidden pride and looked for a surprised expression above the moustache and found it in his eyes and raised eyebrows, the eyebrows, almost as thick as the moustache that said "And you know this how?"

They were both, temporarily, distracted by a piercing scream from what sounded like a very young woman, the screaming and crying coming from the toilets where she was presumably being strip searched and they watched with horror as her, too young to be in a club, boyfriend, on the dance floor, was held back by two men in black as he tried, gallantly, to rescue her. Rebecca ignored the commotion and continued calmly talking to moustache.

"Pink shirt has all the money, back right hand jeans pocket, green jumper takes the order from him and goes to the gents for either a hidden stash or, more likely, a third in the gang. Not even I can see into the gents! Either way there are probably plastic bags with finger prints on, tying the three of them together."

Moustache, held a hand up to politely interrupt her and barked some orders in Spanish to some nearby ninjas and then turned back to Rebecca and lowered his hand "Explain please."

Rebecca smiled. "Sometimes I think it's a gift, sometimes a curse. I used to look after a group of people who had the bodies of sexually mature young adults and the minds of much younger children"

Moustache nodded for her to continue as if he only partly understood.

"I had to have eyes and ears everywhere so, I could be having a conversation with one small group while watching a group the other side of the room and listening to another group behind me. When you do that, day after day for years it sticks. My party trick in the rugby club was to tell people, on my table, what conversations were happening on the surrounding three or four tables. I find now that I can't switch off even when I'm on holiday."

Moustache was impressed and signalled his wife, or perhaps it was a police partner, that they were leaving and they took Rebecca and a still muttering Linda with them. The four jumped into a car and as wife of moustache drove, moustache

looked constantly into the back of the car at
Rebecca as he listened to Linda rabbit on about
the state of her dress as if he was wondering how
such a diverse pair of women could possibly be
friends. What he didn't know, that would have
confused him even more, was that Linda was
complaining bitterly about a dress that she had
borrowed from Rebecca.

The women were dropped off at their hotel for
an enforced but much needed early night and, on
waking in the morning, were advised at reception
that there was a package for Rebecca. They took
the package back up to the room to open it and to
both their surprises it was two thousand euros in
very used tens and twenties with no note of
explanation.

They both knew where the money had come
from and Linda, ever with a one track mind said "I
think you're in there girl"

*... and the wild, money no object, nights after
the drugs bust and getting home, and splitting what
money was left with Linda, I never did get that
dress back, then the phone calls from Geordie
who knew and had worked with 'moustache' and
the interview and training and background checks,
the episode of the Cornwall yacht, smuggling in
the quiet bay on the lonely coastal path and more
money, then selling my parent's house in North
Wales when they died, and the totally unexpected*

large inheritance from them and buying the flat in St. Ives but keeping the valleys house rented out, eventually having enough money for the house with small vineyard in South West France and meeting the Greek property developer on holiday and investing in one of his houses on a small Greek island but foolishly getting too romantically involved and his cheating on me but the villa being in my name and all this ending so recently in my biggest and most important job and not wanting to follow the coverage of the mass murderer on tv or the papers and now travelling to London, and then, this morning, Kitto, dear Kitto, would do anything for me and I should respect him more but do I really want to be a fishwife? This is all just a normal person's life, isn't it? Okay, no."

Having woken early, Brad sat on the end of the bed of his London hotel room, the bed that had reminded him of married life it being far too wide for one person who had never in his life needed six pillows. His head tilted upward, he stared, with his obsessive police trained eyes at the picture on the wall that was, admittedly, almost the same picture that he had looked at in all of the other rooms that he had stayed in at this hotel, but not quite the same. If the dull-painted wall had been blank it would have stood out as being so and this splash of colour was meant to stop guests noticing a blank wall, it was not something to be critically studied. The dots-on-canvas, job-lot copy, an

59

impressionist print of trees and their reflections in a river, was upside down and one supposed reflection without a tree was actually an upside down tree but he couldn't decide whether to mention it or not at reception. Could he explain it without coming over as being a bit weird? Was it a bit weird to even think about mentioning it to reception? Was it something to mention to his therapist to help his session time go by or something to keep to himself forever?

The items he'd bought, the previous day, to save him joining others for breakfast, were emptied, their wrappers, strewn across the worktop table. They would eventually find themselves in the bin that was, in every hotel, too small. He was dressed in his ancient, long legged, washed-out, striped, pyjama bottoms, complete with draw cord and open fly. He had owned them for as long as he could remember, they had been bought for him by his mother when he was in his twenties and he'd never seen a need to replace them but had discarded the button up pyjama top a long time ago. He had travelled, the day before, by train from Newcastle and then by taxi from the train station to the hotel and had remained in his room and would do so until leaving for his meeting with Rebecca, without sightseeing, without leaving his room for any other reason. Unusually for a Londoner, rather than being proud of his city, he hated the place, especially in the summer when it was dry, dusty and full of tourists and memories. To him London was a convenient and central meeting place for him and some of his civilian helpers and nothing else. He hadn't lost his London accent and Rebecca had once explained to him about the habit within Welsh rugby clubs, in which she had grown up, of calling a lad with dead straight hair "Curly" or perhaps "Shorty" if he was six foot six. So cockney Brad was obviously to be called Geordie and the name had stuck in conversations between the two of them especially after Rebecca had found out where he lived.

The hotel room still had its curtains closed with the lights on and the bathroom door was tightly closed with the shower running into the bath. A half-naked Brad was beginning to sweat from the heat emanating from behind the bathroom door that acted as a radiator while it stopped any steam coming into the hotel bedroom to set the smoke alarm off. He had taken the hose of the shower off the wall, placed it in the bottom of the bath like a snake spitting at the bath side and he was running hot water through it at the highest temperature available. At home he always took a bath through choice but there was something about using a hotel bath that made him feel he was sharing the dirt of others so he reluctantly showered but had reasons for always running the hot water through first.

His back dropped onto the bed so he was lying down at a right angle still with his feet on the floor and he stared up at the small crack in the ceiling. The crack wasn't following a rectangular pattern, his investigative brain was calculating, because the plaster was not on rectangular plasterboard and his ceiling, or the floor of the person above, was concrete. This was the way his brain usually coped with boredom, whether he liked it or not, but as the ceiling crack provided no more interest his totally open mind wandered from place to place through the rooms of his past.

... the Met was OK, I was doing... not great, not exceptional but OK, same as the rest of my always average life, sometimes wondered why the hell I was there, like through the riots and looting, why me as a target for stones and bottles, they didn't know me – just my uniform, good money though, overtime, savings in the bank for once but tired all the time. Jane said go abroad for a holiday for once, rest and find each other again, re-learn who her husband was and now she'll never know and we argued, what if the overtime came back while we were away, her saying the force was my real wife and me saying to her that Jimmy had a caravan in Devon, he never went there, wanted nothing in exchange and we could have it for a fortnight and could easily get back to London for the overtime if things kicked off again, so we went to Devon...

Brad had driven from London to Devon knowing that Jane would look for every downside to the holiday that she had wanted to be a holiday abroad but had lost the argument. Brad had been determined to make things work. On arriving at the campsite and unloading the car he'd decided to shower off the morning's sweat, to be fresh to take Jane for a nice lunch. He couldn't have known that the shower in the caravan held a pocket of water. Couldn't have known that the temperature inside the caravan, where windows and doors had remained closed for months, had often reached water heating temperatures. He had heard of people getting legionnaire's disease but that was from cooling towers, not from caravans. He couldn't have had any idea that within the shower, legionella bugs had bred, expanding their little army to millions, waiting for Brad to turn on the spray, to step inside the water and breath in the steam and spray and catch the little bugs in his lungs.

"It started like flu doctor and he put it down to a summer cold but it's just got worse and worse." Jane had to do the explaining as if the doctor was seeing a mother and child as Brad's headache stopped him thinking and speaking and left him with his head in his arms, feeling permanently sick.

The doctor was carrying out his tests, was asking Brad to do things and watching Jane move Brad's body to facilitate. "He's spiked a temperature way above flu; I'm sending you to the local A&E for more tests than I can possibly do here."

Brad wondered why it was that when you got a fever you didn't 'get' a temperature but you 'spiked' a temperature and if he had been able to, he would have asked. By the time that Jane had reached A&E Brad was screaming about headaches. Jane explained to the nurses that he was not the type to normally complain about pain and that she thought it was serious. Brad managed to point, for the consultant, to the right side at the back of his head, above his right eye and the right side of his neck, self-diagnosing himself with a brain tumour that they wouldn't tell him about. At one point he was rolling on the floor in agony.

"Jane, for Christ's sake, if it's a tumour end me now, get it over with, put me out of my agony." This before the injection, before the world closed down, before waking on a hospital ward three days later with tubes and wires everywhere.

"What the f..."

"Brad, it's ok, you're on a ward now." Jane's voice was calming, trying to add some sense to Brad's total confusion.

"Jeez, I remember going to the doctor's with a cold. Did I faint?"

By now nurses had arrived, explained the situation as being a bit like pneumonia, that he was on antibiotics and that he was improving. Their trained voices were calm, reassuring, hypnotic, sleep inducing...

...but then the Met doctor, no return to active service, me, staring at his mouth trying to understand his words with my thoughts in a different world, the world of 'what do I do now,' maybe an admin job he said, then my poor memory and writing everything down, computer lists, all my day to day things in one bag so they couldn't get lost, being told that continually returning to files to remember what's in them and escalating minor things was amplifying my mood and anxiety, and then the over reacting to everything and the job they offered me looking after bloody civilians, based up north but Jane stayed near her folks in London, no kids thankfully and we split up eventually, and hundreds of civilians with on screen maps of where they were and files on them and descriptions of tasks and nothing for me to remember but many admin clerks to help me and The Division called the Public Reserve Group not really existing, officially, feeling like I didn't exist, officially, and the civilians coming up trumps helping the under resourced force and then the statements " a well-meaning member of the public" but the skimming of money to part fund

the department, to reward the civilians, then the villain that had £5k confiscated and got hurt when it was called £3k in court and stupidly kicked up a fuss and...

Brad snapped out of his dream like state on hearing a loud siren outside the hotel window. He jumped up instinctively to see the hoped-for action outside his hotel but then realised that it was only an ambulance disappearing around the corner. Disappointed he looked up and made a decision, took a deep breath in, entered the bathroom, turned off the shower, came back into the bedroom, slammed the bathroom door, breathed out and dressed without a wash.

Leaving the hotel he walked towards the outside café in the park where he had always met Rebecca and other PRG civilians from the south. It was not an especially good place to meet but served its purpose as he knew that he could remember how to get there from the hotel and memory was not his strongest point. He played over the next hour or so in his head and knew that if Rebecca was not seated in the café then he would walk around the perimeter of the park until he saw her seated and would turn up to their meeting after her, but he had no idea why he did this. He carried out a quick self-analysis and decided that his moods were good at the moment with no hint of any oncoming depression.

Usually he was fighting for his departments interests so when a case was completed it was his job to explain, by means of a report, just how his department had helped in the arrest. Usually his report would contain phrases like "PRG pointed the arresting officers in the right direction, saving a great deal of officer's time."

Today things were different. Things were good. He played over in his mind much longer report descriptions such as;

"Although there were few leads being investigated, my department provided the photographic evidence and information that saw the accused reprimanded within 30 minutes of the evidence being gathered. If the accused had not been so quick to exit the scene then my department member would have been making a citizen's arrest at the scene. My department saved the life of the accused's intended victim, secured the crime scene and provided all the initial evidence for the arrest, this evidence being confirmed later by forensic and the findings in the cages at the plumber's yard."

He made a mental note to try and remember these thoughts for long enough to be able to write them down in his notebook at the earliest opportunity, before the thought evaporated.

As Brad arrived at the café he wondered if the wooden, Victorian structure had been repainted in the same colour green since his last visit as it seemed fresher, but he couldn't be sure, perhaps it was the light, perhaps it was his memory. He scanned the group of wooden chairs and tables, Rebecca was not seated, he wondered what time train she had got that morning, and he started his walk around the park unaware that she had left St. Ives the night before.

Chapter 4

Rebecca kept waking out of nightmares and
listening to the noise of metal wheels on metal
track to lull her back to sleep, to a place where she
knew her weird and confused dreams were waiting
for her. She woke the first time, gasping for air and
trying to rip leg-wax tape from her mouth; shortly
after that she woke from a complicated dream
where she had been the only black African in a
restaurant and shit-head sold her into slavery
where she ended up with a fish hook in her cheek,
crawling naked and white again on her roof with
Kitto pulling on one end of a rope like a slave-
master – the other end of the rope tied to the
hook. Later that night she woke while being buried
alive her hands moving rapidly, digging through
the blanket over her and, later again waking while
dreaming that she was burying Linda alive,
shouting at her that it was because she wouldn't
return the dress she'd borrowed – Linda
complaining about the state of her dress as the
earth landed on her. She briefly considered
counselling and just as brusquely, dismissed the
idea.

Eventually the dreams stopped and she woke
before sunrise. She calculated this because there
was no daylight coming through the cracks around
the blind covering the train window, so she

thought for a while and then made the decision to change her phone alarm to six-thirty. She ignored the noise of the wheels on the railway track and went back to sleep until her alarm woke her. She slept solidly this time, comfortable in the knowledge that the alarm would give her an hour of sleep after the train had reached its destination and was no longer moving, then she would have half an hour to dress, which was ample as she would forego queuing for the shared shower and forego also the continental breakfast provided in the ticket price. Being prepared, she had a flannel in her bag that she could use in the small basin in her compartment and also had, in her phone, the address of a good breakfast café, in case she forgot how to get there and had to use her phone's maps to find the postcode.

When oiled, creamed, made up, scented and ready to leave, she threw her mini rucksack over her back and headed off through the echoing noise bubble of muffled train announcements that was Paddington Station and popped into the car engine and horn sounding noise bubble that was a too-fast-moving London.

She was surprised at how busy the pavements of her walk were. There being no workdays or non-working days for Rebecca, she lost track of when others had their enforced nine to five. The morning air was still chilled, especially in the shadows where it was even shivery so, sensibly, she was wearing a very light jacket, more to cover her arms than anything else, but everyone around her, the women especially, were not dressed for the moment but dressed scantily for the heat to come later in the day or for the stuffiness of their office, or their shop counter. Rebecca felt a little bit older than her years, a little bit sensible. The thing that pleased her though, that made her glad that she didn't live here, was the sight of every person around her in a bubble of their own making. A bubble that said I can't see you and you can't see me. That communicating with you would be too great an effort and I can't be bothered. Now the "Hi love, how are you" of St. Ives didn't seem as impersonal as it once had and would gain a bigger return smile when next heard or maybe even a response in words instead of the smile and raised chin.

She smiled to find that her preferred breakfast café was still where it should be, on the expected corner, and took an outside, round, silvery aluminium table, noting that the aluminium chair was dry but that the night-time cold air had affected it and she had to force her back into it to stop it chilling the skin around her spine that had, yet again, been warmed by a rucksack. She ordered from the French menu an Italian cappuccino to drink while she waited for her food, a cheese on toast which she was forced to call a croque monsieur for the waiter's benefit and accompanied this food with a further cappuccino. She followed all this with a hot chocolate that came in a two handled bowl and the taste of the chocolate always felt as though it should be accompanied by a French cigarette, even though she hadn't smoked for years. Reading a free newspaper while people-watching strung the breakfast out to a very French hour and a half until it was time to go to her meeting which, hopefully wouldn't eat too much into her shopping time.

It was only a short walk to the park where she scanned the area and saw Geordie walking around the perimeter, head down and thinking. She tutted to herself, swore that one day, when she had more time, she would also walk the perimeter behind him, to see who gave in first, but today she used a café toilet for the second time in as many hours, took another outdoor café seat, this time wooden and warmed by facing the sun, and sat, wearing sunglasses, with her jacket off and ordering two diet colas and a plate of freshly baked croissant and butter to share, that arrived almost immediately. Brad arrived as if he had smelt the hot croissant and added jam to the order before sitting.

"Not sure you realise the implications of your actions" Brad started, but then realised that he sounded uncaring and that he had to explain "Not talking about the girl, actually still being alive, that's a given. I have word that there's funding to keep our department going for at least a few more years thanks to you and the cracking result."

Rebecca lifted her sunglasses onto the top of her head, revealing the puzzlement in her eyes, Geordie realised that the silence that greeted him meant that it was his turn to speak again. "Of course, the girl's life is the important thing. She's doing well by the way, asking about you." And it felt to him as if they were on neutral ground again for a moment.

Geordie smiled and continued. "Seems he thought these girls were all on the game but they were very high class. No street corner stuff, all by appointment - escort type women, rich businessmen looking for company, that sort of thing. Money up front then to an agency and any talk of sex was purely between the woman and her client, mostly immigrants with no work permits with some bored housewives, hard up for cash, thrown in for good measure. He must have followed them at the end of each of their escort nights. The victims all had a...let's say... an agency head, each of these had a backer who was funded by, let's call him a regional mister big, and there were five Mr Bigs affected by a lack of trade due to your man in a van, each Mr big from a different city. Each one posted an unofficial reward, known to the police and to the dross of the sex world so when collected in they will fund your usual salary, a big bonus and enough to keep my team going for a bit. Not that you'll have to personally wait for the collecting in of course, we can fund that"

Rebecca left a small silence and then said, softly, "Morning Geordie, how are you? You're looking well; going through a good patch I see but still married to the job. All this talk of a girl is making me think of a youngster, a school girl perhaps. Are we talking about the bruised lady that I rescued and her women colleagues?"

Immediately her sarcastic remark was tempered by the thought that she too, was probably seen as married to the job.

The next half hour or so was taken up by small talk in a heady cloud of perfume and after-shave as both disguised the fact they hadn't showered and Brad tried hard to not say the word 'girl' even though he even regarded Rebecca to be a nice looking girl and was puzzled that girls thought that there was some sort of a difference. The croissants, long gone and washed down with further colas, they got down to the business part of their meeting and Brad handed Rebecca a package which she stuffed immediately into the bottom of her rucksack. It went under yesterday's tee shirt, without being opened and he was surprised to receive, in return, the copy memory card containing all the photos from her mission. "Publicity shots for departmental funding attempts" she explained "Plus evidence should anything happen between the local plod shop and the courtroom. I dare say you might use some of them in your report to Mr. Big when you explain what your department is capable of. I'm sure there's a stash of money in my parcel but do you know what that memory card is worth to the Sunday Papers?"

Rebecca knew that these trips to London were an expensive inconvenience for both of them but a necessary evil as all payments have to be made in non-laundered cash, there being no official department to write a cheque and no way that Rebecca could, or would want to, explain a payment by cheque or bank transfer to her accountant or the tax man. Property was the obvious place for the money to go and property abroad easier to hide.

"Yeah, but then the bad guy would get off with a mistrial and you would hate that because you don't do this for the money but to get the bad guys. There's something else though." Brad moved his head closer, his voice softer, smiling while presenting the prize, as if trying to make up for the lack of funds from the newspapers, "My boss asked me about your debrief and you turning down any counselling after your missions. I know we didn't have that conversation this time but I think I know you well enough from previous cases." Brad looked at Rebecca and got the expected nod of agreement, so continued, "His idea, not mine, in the parcel of cash I gave you earlier is a package holiday ticket, two weeks in

Greece, you leave tomorrow night from Bristol, is that ok?"

Rebecca did some quick calculations, shopping this afternoon would now involve new holiday clothes, paid for in cash, an evening meal on the way back to the station, back on the sleeper to St. Ives, wake up in Cornwall tomorrow morning and have a full day to pack and get yet another train to Bristol Airport after stashing the newly acquired twenty pound notes in her Cornwall safe and taking out Euros, of which there were plenty. She very briefly weighed up the nightmares from last night and the offer of counselling against two weeks in the sun before replying.

"Sounds great" she told a waiting Brad, "Tell your boss ta from me. I'll check-in by phone when I'm in the taxi. Oh, by the way, how many of us, like me, were out looking for this guy? What were the odds of one of us coming across any evidence, or even coming across him, especially in daylight?"

Brad gave Rebecca a knowing look, sighed and said, as if for the hundredth time

"You know I can't tell you that. How could I possibly know the answer when the department doesn't exist, I do not exist, you do not exist, this conversation does not exist and the money in your rucksack does not exist? The burying in daylight thing though is curious. We may never know but I am guessing that he got spooked somehow and panicked, had to get rid of your lady a bit sharpish."

Walking back to the park gates they shook hands, professionally, and talked to the drivers of the first two taxis in the queue at the taxi rank, but before getting into the back of the first taxi Brad, possibly because of his euphoria, shouted out

"Bec, more than ten but less than twenty and you are one in a million"

The taxi drivers had no idea what that meant and off the two black cabs went in different directions, Brad directly to his train station, Rebecca to "Shopping", smiling proudly to herself.

It was quite an easy job, in the back of the taxi, to reach inside her rucksack, get inside the pack of cash, find the flight ticket and get it out to investigate. Having a love for small Greek islands and having a villa on a small Greek island thanks to 'shit-head' she was ever so slightly dismayed to read of the huge hotel chain on the just as huge Greek island, but beggars can't be choosers so she went onto the holiday company website to check in for her flight.

Chapter 5

Checking in for the flight was simple, even on her phone in the back of a moving taxi. Rebecca zoomed in to the seating plan to choose an aisle seat, not that there was much choice left. The choice of an aisle seat came naturally to her as a loner, her excuse to herself being that it was just as if she was flying for work purposes and needed to stay anonymous. Pick a window seat and you stand out as a lone female traveller and may attract unwanted conversation. The middle seat is worse; you are possibly splitting up a couple or going to end up sat between two other lonely people. An aisle seat though - an aisle seat indicates that you may have checked in late and your partner or friend or husband could also have an aisle seat elsewhere on the plane. Besides, it makes getting to the toilet easier.

Shopping took on a different twist to the one she'd first expected and planned. Instead of random shopping Rebecca now had a clear focus and the target of finding clothes suitable for a two week holiday in Greece in a posh hotel where you don't exactly wear shorts and a vest over a wet bikini top to dinner. The afternoon was spent flitting from shop to shop and back again and she just about found enough to last the two weeks, paying cash from her new bundle in each shop.

Her overall impression of London shopping, however, was that it had stood still over the years and had let other major cities catch up or overtake. At one point in her expedition she was homesick and wishing she was in the arcades of Cardiff with all the choice that city gave. London, she decided, was not the exciting destination it used to be years before.

Dressing for the moment was still important to Rebecca but sometimes confused her. On tramping around Cornwall for weeks, looking for the murderer, she had worn a dull coloured lumberjack shirt over a high-necked white tee shirt, cargo trousers and hiking boots – not to make a statement but because of the convenience of staying protected from mud and flies. She had known many women who would have found the outfit too masculine, would have had to feminise it, make the tee shirt low necked at the front or find a lumberjack shirt with some pink in it, but this sort of thing didn't bother Rebecca. She understood too the need for control through power dressing and the need for confidence through being comfortable in what you wore but hated adverts that suggested she would have absolutely no confidence without the product being sold. She understood dressing demurely and feminine and the power that it gave you over males but she was not very good at it. In fact, the night of the capture, when she had got blasted on the town, she wanted to feel feminine after weeks of tramping through fields. She'd tried on all her 'come and get me' dresses but ended up in tight jeans and a shirt blouse, the tightness of the jeans, the killer heels and the loosely buttoned blouse being the nod towards looking feminine. Looking back at how she'd arrived back at her flat though, perhaps ditching the dress idea had been a good thing.

What Rebecca couldn't understand, couldn't wear and couldn't see where the power or anything else came from was with the look that was, to her, schizoid in that it was a floral print tiny dress and men's site-working boots. What was that all about?

The most joy she got from shopping these days was from watching, what she termed, the fake women, pretending to be a famous person behind their large sunglasses, hoping people would think *Isn't that what's her name? You know....* Most cities had them but London more than their fair share.

Today they seemed extra false and not only in their nails and hair. Rebecca hoped nobody had her in the same category, a bimbo spending hundreds or thousands on her appearance and pretending it wasn't about attracting a mate. The women around her now reminded her of the women she'd sat and observed in a shopping centre back in South Wales and another of her poems came to mind. This was a poem that she

could remember by heart so mumbled the words
to herself;-
    We forget every mall
    Is built on the bones
    Of a once thriving town
    Now it looks like the rest
    Duplication of greed
    And the Empire Cinema pulled down.

This is how popular I am, as I walk,
My screen to my face,
Expect the next text,
So many texts and so many friends,
But really my phone is a mirror.
Check outward appearance at every poss
I don't think I've looked at my inner.

I am tall and thin and to emphasise this,
I wear very tight clothes and high heels.
My suicide diet just makes me feel good
My Achilles are dead from these six inch heels
My occasional fag kills off muscle in bulk
And 'confident' is how it all feels.

Marvel now at my extensions please,
They really did cost me an arm and a leg
I'll flick them up onto one ear for you
No, not enough glances coming my way
So I'll swap hands with my phone
And tilt my head

And flick them right off again.

My handbag contents are precious to me
Concealer, credit cards, lip gloss
The handle is perched on the crook of my arm
That forces my phone hand right up by my face
You noticed the label on handbag I hope
To have a non-label would be a disgrace.

You'll see I'm not smiling
My face is quite stern but still flat as
I've botoxed my wrinkles.
To smile would be frivolous
Bring me right down
To the 'everyone' people
That I definitely am not.
I long in my heart that an artist on stage
Was the inner of me and
The outer was this that you see.

With her own four, very large, posh branded
carrier bags Rebecca hailed a taxi, told the driver
she was going somewhere in Soho, just to start him
off, and delved into her rucksack for some cash to
pay him with and to retrieve her old spiral bound
notebook. She had always intended to eat Greek
before her sleeper train took her back to St. Ives,
even before her free Greek holiday was
mentioned. The reason behind that was that she'd
eaten Greek the last time she'd been in London

and had heard, in the restaurant a quarter of what might have been possibly an interesting snippet, maybe, almost. It was that vague and trivial a conversation but enough for her to have made a note. Anyway, she remembered that the food was good and that was more important. She flicked through her notebook, found the note, gave the taxi driver the street name in the note and tried to decipher the pencil scribble in front of her.

"*Two guys, owners? Serve. Big, small, big more boss, small talking about crate of wine into country, big not happy, argue or just shouty Greek conversation? Use word danger by big, small says money. Bring wine? Dictionary way home – not crate, word is box. Dangerous wine boxes for money? Greek improver course for me?*"

In her memory the note had been vague but it hadn't seemed quite that vague, time being a huge distorter of the facts as usual. She was hungry anyway so made her way from the taxi drop-off, walked down the street to the restaurant and sat near the counter at the rear, piling the carrier bags on the two seats opposite her and placing her rucksack on the seat next to her, totally claiming the table for four even though the restaurant was practically empty.

Rebecca sat staring at the tourist designed menu, full of what Greeks would regard as 'only on feast-day' dishes that Brits will have eaten every night on holiday and will, the owners hope, want to order again, now, to bring back happy memories. Perhaps not strangely, the menu had completely changed since her last visit. The food was much the same but the layout of the menu was much improved. It now gave a history of the family living on the Greek island of Pothanaramos, why they came to London and how they capture the flavour and history of that island and lovingly place that flavour and the history into their food, for your enjoyment. There was a not very extensive wine list, each wine having been produced on the island though and a claim that the food and wine was authentic to their homeland island, despite the fact that it was food that, Rebecca knew, could be found anywhere in Greece. She decided on a single starter course of orektika for one, for now and contemplated her ingrained, but some would say strange, habits with taxis and Greek food.

She had asked the taxi to stop at the end of the street and had walked to the restaurant, much as the taxi had dropped her off near, but not at, her flat the other day in St. Ives. Was this paranoia? Was there the slightest chance that somebody would be asking the taxi driver "Hey, buddy, where did she get off?" Was her life becoming melodramatic? The habit of ordering Greek food in a single course, and then asking for the menu back to choose the next course, came from her ex-lover, shit-head (really, I still can't call him by his real name after all this time?) who taught her the art of ordering single courses on many small romantic Greek islands. His deep voice and Greek accent was now flooding over her brain. "Number one, Greek food is put on the table for everyone and anyone to eat in whatever order they want. Order an English style starter and main course and it could all come at the same time. Number two, if you have ordered a starter and in to the taverna comes a loud person who wants to tell the whole place what he did that day, you can finish your starter and then order your main at the taverna down the road." Shit-head had learnt his English in America along with his skills in real estate, he disliked Americans but would never tell her why and, of course, he pretended to love them while taking their money in exchange for his newly built villas on cheaply bought land. Rebecca had a fantastic deal on her Greek property paying only what it had cost her lover to build it, without his profit, a deal that now felt like "The deeds are totally in your name, pay less than half of the real property value and sleep with me for a couple of months until I get bored with you and we'll call it quits." She had the property, she had the memories, but at what overall price to her feelings about relationships, feelings that to be honest, had not been that great anyway.

Rebecca was brought back to reality by the waiter asking her for her order so she snapped out of her thoughts and ordered the orektika, purposely struggling over the pronunciation and giving a smile of apology, as if it is the first time she had attempted a Greek word. Of course the waiter asked if she would like a drink and she ached to ask for a tsipouro, but that would have been far too Greek and could have alerted the waiter to a possible understanding of his language so, she ordered a gin and tonic, sighed and lapsed back into drifting memory.

Which island were we on, there were so many in that heady period when I pretended to be excited as I allowed him to try and impress me with his money and travel to keep his egotistical brain happy. The taverna was at the very top of the steep hill, up hundreds of breath sapping steps from the harbour and I was praying I wouldn't be dripping with sweat at the top. The seating area was in the open air, in the middle of a ruined castle, overlooking the harbour. Shit-head ordered tsipouro for us both, and explained that it was a type of ouzo, and with it came a snack for us to romantically share. Every time another drink was ordered the snack became bigger and I remember thinking that the last snack was more like a full meal. The conversation from the locals got louder, the atmosphere more electric. I was shocked when I suddenly realised that there were no tourists present, this was a night for the youth of the village and I was the only non-Greek present, which was a situation I'd never been in before. Without

*warning some of the tables emptied and two large
circles of dancers formed; a circle of women at
one end of the taverna, a circle of boys at the other
end. As they danced, shit-head leant over and said
"authentic....not done for tourists" but my eyes
were glued on the circle of women and the
paradox between the very ancient dance and their
very modern clothes. A woman broke from the
circle and stood, demurely in the centre, losing the
steps of her friends and dancing to herself with
hands clenched in front of her, face looking down
in sweet embarrassment, her friends whooping and
cheering. Then the boys cheered as one of their
kind stood in the middle of his circle, his friends
stepping around him. I remember shouting into
shit-head's ear, without taking my eyes off the
dancers "Are they engaged now or something?"
And he laughed out loud, almost breaking the
spell I was under "You are too romantic" he
scoffed, and I thought "I want to be the woman in
the circle and I want you to be the boy circled over
there".*

*It wasn't to be. It was only about a month after
that beautiful night that I got back to our hotel
room after my shopping trip catamaran to Athens
had been cancelled by bad weather, found him in
bed with a wannabe Mrs. Shit-head and had
walked out of his life forever. It was an
embarrassing search for my passport, clothes and
bag and I remember telling the woman, in English*

that she possibly didn't understand, that she was
young enough to be the daughter of shit-head and
good luck to her and the next one after her. Shit-
head could not get out of bed, probably because of
an embarrassingly enlarged member, the shouted
words from him "It's not what you think" ringing
in my ears as I left, laughing loud enough for them
both to hear.

Rebecca jumped as her plate was placed in front of her, she took a reality check, made sure she had not been crying and thanked the waiter while trying to breathe deeply and regain some composure. Was it the pungent aromas of Greek cooking that transported her back to Greece in her mind every time she allowed that mind to wander?

While nibbling at the small taster pieces and drinking her gin she watched the waiter return to the desk and wondered if he was the 'big' or the 'small' in her notebook. Then 'big' came out from the kitchens making 'small' look smaller.

In came a man and looked around, said hi to 'big' and they exchanged conversation to the point where it became obvious that this was not a customer. From Rebecca's viewpoint he looked like he was your average on-trend bloke. He walked the length of the taverna without Rebecca looking directly at him but the corner of her left eye told her that his hair wasn't oiled back, it was greasy, his designer stubble was not designed, it was the laziness of not shaving for a week, his clothes were not shabby chic but just shabby. This was a shady character. She looked down at her plate as 'shady character' went out towards the kitchen area presumably to see 'small' who had disappeared in that direction. After five minutes 'shady character' returned from the kitchen with a wine box labelled Merlot as if the establishment was an off-licence. Out of the corner of Rebecca's eye she saw 'small' return to the cash desk with a carrier bag that he showed to big. If that bag was full of currency then it would have bought many, many boxes of wine.

'Big' was seated near the door, his bum on the back of a chair, his feet on the bit you sit on, as if waiting for new customers and, having received the raised bag 'OK' signal from 'small' said to 'shady character', in English "really good wine, you will enjoy."

'Small' looked up but Rebecca was looking down at her plate and only lifted her head slightly to take a drink and look straight ahead, ensuring that she looked nowhere near 'small' and looked totally disinterested in what was going on. She took another mouthful of food and was deep in thought, trying to remember the many wine books she had bought when she first started travelling to Greece, the Greek wine books with the long, unpronounceable at first, Greek grape names. Things had obviously changed over the years and French grapes like merlot were now being grown on the island but where, oh where, were those books now?

Her main course was uneventful with regard to taste but gave her the opportunity to see the menu again, to confirm that merlot was not on the wine list as a bottle or a single glass. Rebecca had never had a pudding course in a Greek taverna, they were always disappointing. She preferred to walk to the local sugar and pastry shop if she was in Greece for cake but there was nothing like that around where she was now.

Wanting to know more about this taverna, after settling her bill in cash, she crossed the road, looked up to the roof of the restaurant and took note of a chimney stack on the right hand side with buddleia shrub growing out of the side of it. Walking down the street she counted another seventeen chimney stacks before she turned left and then left again. Walking up a lane used for deliveries she looked up, counted again seventeen chimney stacks and could see again the buddleia bush and knew that she was at the back of the restaurant where she has just eaten. Looking into the yard she saw the back door open and suddenly reality hit her. Rebecca felt very exposed. She was instantly recognisable to 'big' and to 'small' and standing out ever so slightly with her designer carrier bags she knew she couldn't get too close or get seen. She was in a dark lane and looking like a Christmas present to any mugger.....or worse. She turned and noticed the distance to the street but the walk back to civilisation was a lot quicker both for her footsteps and for her heartbeat and this time did not include counting chimney pots. She had made herself vulnerable for no gain. Geordie would not have been impressed. Just as she thought she was safe and emerging at the end of the lane, she saw movement out of the corner of her eye and turned towards it instinctively, and saw in a yard similar to the one she has just visited, 'shady character' with a needle in his arm. He looked up but was hopefully too 'out of it' or soon would be, to either recognise Rebecca or to even care. It confirmed a lot of her suspicions. If he was a runner, stealing from his boss, then he had better be au-fait with amounts of pure heroin to use, enough to be out of it and hang on to his bosses wine box, or his boss would kill him if the heroin didn't. Of course, he could be using his own stash of 'cut many times' heroin with his bosses parcel still intact.

Running now to the bright lights of the main street, Rebecca hailed a taxi, sat in the back and breathed out loudly, with relief but also with the realisation that she was sweating. "Paddington rail station please" were the only words she managed to get out on the journey and when they arrived at Paddington she waited in a café for her sleeper train, deep in thought, based around the contents of the wine box, was it heroin and if so was it a hundred percent. Was 'shady character' stealing from his boss and, if he was stealing pure heroin then would he be alive in the morning? Was there a way to find out if he died overnight? Logically, if 'shady character' had done this run a number of times, he would know how much to use and how to steal it without his boss knowing. Rebecca wished that she had the guts to have followed 'shady character' to his boss's home but even if she hadn't been laden down with her shopping, she knew it would have been too dangerous. Perhaps what should have been more important to her than the life of 'shady character' was what would have happened if she had come face to face with him, high on heroin, desperate for money, her with a money stash and bags of posh clothes?

Feeling unusually vulnerable she sent a text to Kitto *"Changed plan. Holiday two weeks Greece" Drink when I get back? Bec"*.... Send.....whoosh.

Then thought *"me feeling vulnerable, first thought Kitto. Why?"*

When she arrived back in St. Ives, all she had to do was get her passport, pack a combination of her new and some older clothes and get yet another train back up to Bristol to get her plane. This she dragged out slowly, having the whole day to accomplish the tasks and getting a little fed up with being on the move. Eventually though, she was on her way to the train station in St. Ives.

This time Rebecca was dragging a suitcase

noisily behind her up Fore Street and over the cobbles with each wheel banging into each cobble. Each banging sound reverberated off the walls of the shops in this narrow street and had the advantage of letting the crowds know that she was on her way and that they should part like the red sea. Yet again, she promised herself that when she had time, if ever she had time, she would invent and market and sell a case with soft rubber tyres that were quiet.

Bristol airport was full of holiday makers who had spent more than they could really afford on their holiday in an attempt to relax from their everyday lives but, at the same time, they were stressed about travelling and so they were marking the transition from work to play with alcohol. Rebecca, on the other hand, was tired of travelling, tired of trains and taxis, not looking forward to trying to sleep on the plane flight, fed up of not knowing what day it was.

People-watching was a bit boring for her among those waiting at the airport gate. Rebecca was dressed-down and comfortable in very baggy light striped trousers, gathered at the ankle, sandals and a cheesecloth top and would not have looked out of place in the nineteen-sixties. In comparison, there was one very tall couple who were not worth studying as they were dressed, not for travel but in their finery, wishing to stand out as having money, him in his blazer, her in her jewellery. Those that stand out are not worth watching, she decided long ago, as, to be beyond the law you have to meld into the background.

There was the usual rush to get onto the plane, as if there were not enough seats and the people thought that they should claim the seat numbers on their boarding cards before the seats disappeared. Everyone settled in their seats but they were still edgy because the plane hadn't yet taken off. The safety briefing happened with everyone staring blankly and pretending to listen and then take-off eventually happened with everyone finally relaxing knowing that nothing now could stop them getting to their holiday destination. Rebecca settled down with a blackout mask and earbuds and might as well have written "Get Lost" on her forehead as it would have given the same message.

She was surprised to find that she slept the whole journey but still yearned to sleep while she wasn't in motion, this being the third night in a row of sleep while travelling preceded by a drunken sleep that was preceded by weeks sleeping in a tent. Waiting for the plane to come to a standstill, then standing to get her hand luggage and queueing to leave the plane she could see that her fellow travellers were more tired than she was and as she stepped out onto the aircraft steps she was fully prepared for the heat to smash her in the face, even though the night was dark. It was that smash to the face that triggered a switch in her brain that turned on 'Greek mode' that slowed her motions down, giving her a 'don't care' attitude that calmed her brain down. The Greek word that sprung to mind was 'avrio', tomorrow, it will get done tomorrow.

It was baggage reclaim though that Rebecca enjoyed watching as she casually stood back from the baggage belt, waiting for gaps in the crowds after some of the cases had been removed. At this point she felt Greek and felt like a local watching a bunch of crazy tourists. There was a definite male to female split to the chores to be undertaken, harping back to caveman days. The women sent their men out to hunter-gather the luggage. The men were keen eyed and could spot their luggage because the women who had packed the cases had described what the cases looked like to them. The men were strong and could lift their prey off the luggage belt. Often a male hunter would return with one case and offer it to the female, smiling in ritual, seeking praise, before returning to the belt to find a second case.

Outside the airport the male was left with the cases while the nesting female of the species claimed two seats on the transfer coach, her new found territory being offered to the male for him to share once he has completed his task of making sure the cases were in the luggage compartment under the coach. Of course, Rebecca, being on her own was playing both parts.

On arriving at the holiday hotel the female would take the male's prey and carve the joint, dividing the contents into various drawers and cupboards, looking after those contents through the holiday until it was time for her male to, once again, strongly lift the cases onto the coach.

Arriving at the huge, non-Greek, international feeling, could be anywhere in the world, hotel, in the early hours before dawn, most went straight to bed, waking after a few hours to struggle through a late buffet breakfast, wandering, bleary eyed, not knowing where anything was to be found and then they lay-out in the sun, hating the fact that they were a lot whiter than those on the second week of their holiday.

Rebecca chose a parasol and two beds next to the pool, deciding to stay close to the hotel and maybe find the beach tomorrow. The spare towel over the spare bed shouted that she might not be alone. The large sunglasses shielding her face from view, shouted that she may be asleep. The ear buds in her ears that lead to her phone that was playing no music whatsoever were shouting that she did not want to converse with anyone. In fact, even though no sound was coming through her ear buds, if anyone said something to her, for instance a waiter offering coffee, she would hear them, remove one ear bud, say pardon, answer briefly with a smile and replace the ear bud to show that the conversation was closed.

Rebecca couldn't switch off from what she regarded as a full time job as, with a place to live in Cornwall, France and Greece, life was as if she was on a permanent holiday anyway, but at the same time being a civilian watcher, helping out the good guys. Behind her sunglasses she was people-watching and listening. The only thing she came up with, however, over the whole day, was the fact that 'ordinary' women, like her, aided sun bathing by tying their hair back or up into a bun with a scrunch, without getting off the sun-bed, while those who were aiming for the anorexic look, in the minutest of bikinis, did the same but, had to stand up to do it. With arms above their heads, stretching their bodies for an even more anorexic look, they made three attempts at their hair before sitting back down again and then went through the same ritual, hourly. Boredom and perhaps the minutest hint of jealousy set in. Relaxing was not the Rebecca way. She had to do something and fast. Skinny women displaying was not going to satisfy her brain for two weeks. Hoping there was a tie up between the London taverna, the island of the taverna owner's home and also with the winery on the island of Pothanaramos, Rebecca decided she couldn't sit around the pool for one more hour.

From her room she sent a text. "*Paraskevi, is my villa ready for a visit? I may be there tomorrow, maybe next day. Where is Pothanaramos? Clear out any boyfriends!!! Hope you are well. Rebecca"*

A not so friendly, hurried text back, about an hour later, set the mood of the island *"Bec, no boyfriends, but thanks for use of villa – used when argue with baba and mama, less tourists, less money from taverna, immigrants, things are bad but your villa clean, tidy and with bowl of fruit waiting for you. Love, Paraskevi."*

Chapter 6

At the hotel reception, the following morning, the many desk clerks each had a queue to deal with and were variously dealing with complaints about non sea views, broken light bulbs and air conditioning that would not pick the exact temperature deemed necessary by the occupant. Rebecca provided a distraction for them with something more interesting.

"Hi, I'm in room 204 and I've just learned that a friend of mine, back in Athens, has become ill. I will leave today to visit her. Please keep my room open until the end of my holiday, tell the maid no need to clean every day, I will ring to tell you when I will be back and will leave most of my luggage in the room."

The hotel arranged a taxi to the port and Rebecca got a ticket, not to Athens but to the small island of Skopelos. From there she would be able to get another high speed catamaran to her island home and her villa which was already fully wardrobed and had all the surveillance gear that she had sent, piece by piece, to the islands post office for picking up by Paraskevi. The villa also had a safe stuffed with Euros from rewards from past encounters with the bad guys, should she need a top-up.

On the catamaran she received a text from Geordie and longed for the days before mobiles.

"Why left hotel? Who ill? When return hotel?"

Nosey B, thought Rebecca as she sent a stupidly sarcastic text back.

"Sorry, no signal and money run out on phone. Will answer your text when able."

After island hopping with high speed catamaran journeys that felt like commuting bus journeys, she arrived at her villa complex in a taxi. She picked up her key from the man at the booth at the gated entry after waking him from his nap, passed the immaculately manicured lawns in the central area around the villas, entered the cool of her own villa, lay on the bed and thought; *day trains, night trains, taxis, planes, coaches, catamarans, I need to sleep while not moving. I need to stay in one place for a while. I must force myself to relax and wash out the adrenalin buzz of the capture of the mass murderer.* Although it was mid-afternoon and hot, she went to the drawer where she knew her pyjamas were, chose a light blue, lightweight, silk set, changed and dropped off to sleep on top of the bed, immediately.

The noise of the curtains being pulled back and the sun streaming in without the cries of sea gulls made Rebecca confirm in her head, without opening her eyes, that she was in Greece, in her own bed in her own villa, had crawled under the sheets without waking, had slept the night through, that Paraskevi had let herself in and had hopefully organised breakfast and that all was right with the world. Until a very frantic, hurried voice...

"Rebecca, how are you? It has been too long. I have missed you. Things are bad here but, first, breakfast. Your yoghourt and honey here, on this plate your fruit, coffee in the pot here and a confession please that while you were gone I stole your clothes and washed them to put them back."

"Borrowed" corrected Rebecca, lifting her head up from the pillow and looking at Paraskevi with one eye. She grabbed a pillow, threw it at the headboard, lifted herself up and stuffed another pillow between her back and the headboard "You borrowed my clothes and put them back, and that's ok with me."

The two phrases, unspoken, that went through Rebecca's head were 'hand wash only' and 'dry clean only', wondering if Para's English was good enough to understand those phrases. Bec and Para had an agreement that Rebecca would correct Paraskevi's English and have corrected Greek in return – without laughter or making fun.

"You are not angry? Things are tough in the taverna" Paraskevi offered in explanation. "Please to eat your yoghourt while I explain. The immigrants came to some islands and they were begging outside the tavernas. The holidaymakers could not eat and watch people starve at the same time. It is understandable. Many bought food from supermarkets, ate some and gave some to the immigrants. When they went home they told their friends, now only a few come here to Greece and anyway you English worried about buying Euros to find Greece going back to the Drachma so all is bad and, by the way, not your underwear or bikinis, I didn't steal these things. And I am puzzled why you have so many bikinis?"

"It's ok."

Rebecca smiled to try and break the serious face of her friend who was talking nineteen to the dozen as if she were conversing in Greek and jumping from subject to subject as Rebecca now remembered her friend's curious habit. The smile remained as it had been a while since her taste buds had experienced the sharp taste of real, unsweetened, Greek yoghurt, contrasting with the sweet taste of local Greek honey, all in one glorious mouthful.

"The whole world knows what has been happening; we have watched it on the television news".

The conversation continued but Rebecca was thinking about all those bikinis. Not an obsession with clothes, well not totally anyway, but part of the job. She knew that if she sat on the same beach every day for a fortnight, listening to surrounding conversations, and wearing a different bikini each day, had a different colour towel each day, wore hair down, partly up, hair up, small sunglasses, large sunglasses, medium sunglasses – then she could fool ninety percent of women and one hundred per cent of men into thinking that she was a different person on each day of the fortnight.

Paraskevi was still looking worried, still begging forgiveness.

"I have told you in the past, Baba wanted a son to take on the taverna, Mama could only give him me, a mere woman. You told me to fight against his ideas for more taverna business, the short black skirts and the low white blouses. Our arguments just made him angry, made him hate me more. I am afraid that was when I found the clothes in your wardrobe that I stole that I thought would bring in more custom to our taverna. It was like I wore white blouse, black skirt all my life, living in a black and white movie. When I stole, sorry, borrowed your colourful clothes I felt powerful, I felt like more than me, not so much for the colour of the clothes but their style – I will explain in a bit. Now when nobody eats in any taverna it seems to Baba that it is my entire fault. Rebecca, black and white, colourful, if I served food naked like I was born, it would be no good if there are few people on the island who want to eat at any taverna. Our island is not affected by immigrants so much as the islands close to Turkey and near the Greek mainland, that is their route to go to the rest of Europe, but you, you at home in Britain hear Greece and think it is all one little area, the same place.

Rebecca looked down and thought of a reply.

"I don't care about the clothes Para. I bet they look better on you anyway". They both laugh and this seemed to break the ice.

"Rebecca, since we last met, I have learnt subtle. I think that is the right word, and I learnt it from one man who was in three couples. I don't think I have told you this story".

Rebecca gave a questioning face and nodded her head from side to side and then settled back for what sounded like it was going to be a long story, the tray still on her lap.

"I captured the six, that is three couples, when they walked along the road, and were ignoring all the pleas to go into other tavernas, or pleas to just look at menus, it is the same thing. I captured them by not hassling them but by dragging a table for two up to a four, making it a six. They were impressed and came in to eat with me. They came many times and, after a while, they were brave enough to even move their own tables. One day they stayed late and asked me to join them – I had mostly cleared up so said yes to try and improve my English and to hope that they would keep coming to eat with me.

They told me that they didn't know each other before the holiday, that they had met and had become friends but lived in different places so would not be friends after the holiday. The women told me that they sunbathed with no bikini tops, on the beach, and now that they had a tan, they each wore very low cut tops to dinner to show off their brown skin. One woman told me the difference between English and Greek men. She said English men would pretend not to notice your boobs in a low cut top but would glance now and then but a Greek man, especially old men, would just, very openly, stare at your boobs. Then one of the men told me something I have never forgotten. He said that he had conducted an experiment on the women from the other two couples. He said that on the beach he had talked to both of them and that because they had no tops he could obviously see all of their boobs, the top, the bottom, their nipples, everything and the women did not care. Tonight, over dinner, he talked to each of them again and this time glanced at their cleavage in their low tops. Each woman automatically put their hand over their cleavage to hide it, even though that same man had seen the whole of their boobs only hours earlier. The women were puzzled and discussed that maybe it was because of the different setting or maybe it was because a little glance was sexier than looking at the whole thing.

From that day I stopped wearing my white blouses, with buttons missing, where my boobs were on show all the time and started wearing your bigger tops that mostly covered my boobs except when I leant over. Of course I already had the thing where, to clear plates, I would stand next to the woman in a couple and bend down towards the man for him to look, so I was already earning good tips when the man paid, but I think the 'subtle' brought in more repeat business".

Rebecca was nodding through all of this, agreeing with Para all the time. She was proud of her friend and her analysis of the male brain but upset that she was forced to act this way. She was busy moving from one breakfast item to the next and hadn't realised how hungry and thirsty she was. She poured a thick, powdery, black coffee into a small cup while talking and set it aside to settle, joining in the conversation to give Para a break.

"You've told me before how your father, your Baba treats you like an object to make money. You said once that when your parents die you may not be allowed to carry on the taverna."

Paraskevi looked sad and, without thinking, tidied the room as she spoke, arranging the cushions on an arm chair near the window.

"It is already now decided it will go to my cousin Yiorgo, only a man can be in charge of a taverna, it seems. Worse, there is talk of me marrying Yiorgo, yes, my cousin, they say, if not, then what will I do. My only escape would be to marry someone else, someone who has another business and to cook for them for the rest of my life. Rebecca, I am tired of not being me, tired of wearing clothes that will decide if people come back to eat with us again."

Rebecca knew that things were bad for her friend and housekeeper but felt guilty that she has not kept in touch more as Para's life had gone downhill.

"Have you discussed this with your Mama, does she realise that things are changing for women in Greece, even on small islands?"

Paraskevi blew out with her lips with her cheeks both flapping at the same time as only

Mediterranean people can, stopped tidying, sat on the end of the bed and explained.

"Mama told me, in answer to my complaints to her, what life had been like for her. You know? Like, oh, so you think you've got it bad. She told me that when she was a woman you could walk onto any beach and know immediately who the Greek women were. They would be wearing one piece bathing costumes, always plain black. The tourist women too would wear one piece also but it would be just a bikini bottom with no top bit and the back of the bottoms going up the bum crack. Like me she was taken out of school at fifteen years to work. Later she was betrothed by family arrangements to Baba and worked in his parent's taverna, our taverna now, while Baba did his national service. When Baba came back to the island he was a changed man, more confident, bigger and, how you say, more muscles. Mama liked this and was proud of her man through the first winter but remembers, in the summer, talking to Baba on the beach but Baba was looking over her shoulder all the time at the almost naked tourists. Eventually she found that as she was cooking all day, he was drinking beer and coffee with his friends and when it was time to serve tourists, she would dish out and plate up and watch Baba flirt with the tourist women and disappear after the taverna was closed. On the one time she complained to him he told her there was no worry, that the tourist women took a tablet not to become pregnant and that perhaps Mama was also taking that tablet. She told me she wanted to go somewhere away from Baba but had nowhere to go. Then she laughed and told me that Baba still flirts but the women laugh behind his back now at his big belly.

So you see Rebecca, me marrying Yiorgo so that we can keep the taverna going as a pension for Baba and Mama is a leap forward in their eyes and I should be grateful, but, of course, it doesn't feel like that."

It was at that point that Rebecca decided to rescue her friend from oblivion and vowed that she would try to include her in what would hopefully become a joint adventure.

"I have a plan for all that Para, I have been thinking about you. I will eat this glorious fruit and then we will find an answer." Rebecca was smiling and eating at the same time. "Did you look up Pothanaramos for me?"

"I didn't have to, it is the island of my mother's grandfather's birth and upbringing and I have been twice to the bone house where his bones are to pay thanks to him on behalf of Mama who cannot, or will not, travel. It is a small island with some few people who holiday and not so much hit by immigrants."

"When can we go?" Rebecca was excited. "When can you show me the island?"

Expecting a negative answer and excuses as to why her friend couldn't leave the taverna, Rebecca continued.

"You said business in the taverna is bad, what if you tell your Baba that I will pay you as a guide and translator"

Paraskevi was excited but shocked into thinking about the proposition of leaving the taverna, but to leave the island with trade so bad. She looked undecided in a Greek, negotiating sort of way, so Rebecca continued.

"I don't know what money you are making for your Baba at the moment in the taverna but what if you told him that the crazy Welsh woman, who pays you to clean her villa, would pay a hundred Euros a day. Our deal would be two hundred a day and you can hide the difference in my villa somewhere until you need it. And you can have a week or two living just for you, not for him!"

Rebecca knew that things were moving forward. If her hunch was right then they could be in the money. If wrong and there was no drug smuggling ring, then they would, at least, have a good holiday together. The two hundred a day and the cost of the next hotel would be Rebecca's only major holiday costs, her flights having been paid for by Geordie and his department.

Paraskevi skipped down the road to put the proposition to her father while Rebecca stripped off silk pyjamas and entered the pool that was totally enclosed by her villa and totally private. With walls of rooms around three sides of the infinity pool and a sea view on the fourth side, skinny dipping was possible and her villa had the same layout as all the other luxury villas in the complex that were put together by Shit-head and mostly owned now by Brits, Germans and Americans who had seen their investments plummet in price, even faster than the Greek economy went down. After an hour of feeling the cool water against her naked skin as she swam repeats of one length on the top, one underwater, she showered, dressed and reached for her ringing phone that had "Para" on it with a picture of her friend.

"He says I can go with his blessing, well, not in so many words, he says I am a useless piece of poo and might as well strangle a stupid Brit for any money we can grab rather than sit on my bum - in Greek it means the same thing."

Rebecca was thrilled. "Para, come up to the villa with some changes of clothes, no, borrow or steal some of mine, you choose. I have to explain to

111

you where we are going and why and explain some of the stuff I keep in my villa, OK?"

When Para arrived they giggled like childish girls at the thought of going on an adventure together. Paraskevi went to the glass doored wine-cave fridge unit and extracted a bottle of white and opened it, pouring two glasses as if she was in her own home and Rebecca, once again, felt like the visitor, her mind jumping back to Kitto and his coffee making. Rebecca wondered how many times her everyday quaffing wine had been consumed and then replenished from the local supermarket. She made a mental note to later look at the vintage years on the bottles and then she called a halt to the frivolity and started to explain her thoughts.

She told Para about the taverna in London and everything that happened there without telling her anything about her past or the civilian post she held. After much questioning by Paraskevi about whether Rebecca was police or not, and even more questions about the strange surveillance gear that she had collected at her villa, pretending to be satisfied that Rebecca was a bored civilian looking for some excitement and money in her life, she told Rebecca everything she knew about Pothanaramos.

"Taste of Pothanaramos is not just the name of your taverna in London; it is the English translation of the name of the winery on the island. The island is poor and the winery was built with money from rich European countries that have now decided that they want their money back, even though it strangles and kills my country but that is another story. Anyway, it is a co-operative and nearly all the grapes grown on the island, in gardens and small plots, (there are no big vineyards) are taken to this winery, that is owned by the island, where they make red and white wines, some for export to mainland Greece but most to be drunk locally in the tavernas there and on surrounding islands. I think if your London taverna has these wines then they import them privately to make a connection to the island on their menu. Some bottles, of course, go back to the people who grew the grapes for them to drink throughout the year.

It would be easy for people smugglers to get refugees to the island from Turkey as the authorities concentrate on the bigger islands. Refugees from Afghanistan for instance would be interviewed and placed in a small camp area before being sent to a holding camp on a bigger island, before being sent back to Turkey. Perhaps if they cannot pay the smuggler who gets them to Greece then the bill would be to take drugs with them and hand them to someone on the island instead of paying the smuggler in cash. We have heard on our island that this is something that happens – but you know us Greeks and our rumours and gossip, and anyway, the drugs do not affect us, they go north to richer countries."

"All makes sense" Rebecca was nodding and thinking. "But where does the wine come into it. Can you dilute drugs into the wine? Would it be detectable? Would it taste? I am fed up of moving from place to place Para but I feel another journey coming on."

Before Para left for her home Bec said she would have another skinny dip before bed and Para joined her, admitting that it was not the first time that she had been naked in Bec's pool. Rebecca could see, from Para's figure, that she would look good in her borrowed clothes. Para's hip and waist size were similar to Bec's but because Para was shorter the curve between waist and hips was accentuated and sexier. Her boobs too, of similar size to Bec's looked a lot younger, more pert, almost a false look although to be false would be impossible. The cool water eventually negated the effects of the wine and the women parted company a lot cooler and ready for sleep.

The following day on the catamaran trail that would eventually get them to Pothanaramos, Paraskevi explained to Rebecca that Pothanaramos was the type of very small island where if one person knew a fact then the whole island knew the same fact within an hour. So, when they docked and entered the first and only port-side café for iced frappé Para struck up a conversation with the waiter and, in fast Greek that Rebecca could only just about follow, explained that she had come to venerate the bones of her great grandfather on her mother's side and that her cousin from Britain whose family no longer spoke Greek, had come along too to join in the tradition. Para found from the waiter the name of the best hotel on the island which, of course, happened to be owned by the waiter's uncle and he organised the taxi, owned by his cousin, to get them there and, before long the women were unpacking and arguing over wardrobe space. Rebecca saw her clothes evenly spread over both sides of the wardrobe and asked Para "Para, you used to be a different shape to me, how come my clothes fitted you so well?"

A smiling Paraskevi answered.

"Mama does not cook so much now as there are fewer tourists so I am no longer eating left over scraps and running between tables. I am eating supermarket food and sitting on my bum so I become as huge as you"

"Big" Rebecca corrected her quickly "You become as big as me not as huge as me. Huge is too big, like an elephant."

"Ok, big. But before that, lots of safety pins. Also you wear your skirts and dresses too short for our age so I am shorter and then they look more respectable. Rebecca, when do we go to the winery?"

Rebecca wished that Greek people and Para in particular, were not quite so honest in their answers. Feeling as if she was a huge woman who dressed too young for her age she also wished that Para's semi-insults didn't end with a deflecting question.

"We have to be patient, we have to stay safe, I want to listen to what is being said on the beach and then we can go and have a look. I think the little village we are in is in a great spot, away from the coast and within walking distance of all the beaches and also the winery, which is great. The only down side is that whatever move we make will be known by everyone in the village. Perhaps we will split duties between the beach and the winery, perhaps I have a plan."

Chapter 7

It was approaching midday so the sun was making small but intense shadows with striking contrasts against the whitewashed wall of the two storey house. Petros wanted to trust the timber of each rung of the ladder that he was near the top of but was made suspicious by the two very new replacement rungs with little paint spill on them. The smell of the paint he had used to re-colour the first floor window shutters was filling the air with its heady linseed smell and he still didn't understand why his friends had made him buy linseed oil to thin the thick blue too-old-really paint when he had been sure that cheap olive oil would have done the trick and smelt less potent. When he danced he stared at the ground, at one with the planet that he lived on. When he used the group's ladder he was at one with the tree that made the wood that was crafted into the ladder by some ancient and unknown carpenter. This ladder had a history. It was the ladder that was shared by the eight boys in his group and used by whoever needed to use it, whoever happened to have work that required 'the ladder.' Perhaps one of their fathers had once borrowed it and the owner didn't want it back.

His thoughts were deep; his head full of linseed, the sun burnt his neck, when...

"Why are you measuring my window and wearing sunglasses Petros when we have already agreed a price?"

Kyria Colos had suddenly appeared at the window where Petros was perched, where he had painted the shutters in a blue colour that matched the colour of the sea, contrasting with the whitewashed walls, the walls that were reflecting the strong midday sun and forcing the wearing of sunglasses and which mirrored the white of the caps of the waves. She had no thought that her sudden, unexpected appearance could have sent Petros tumbling to the ground. *Good to keep these youngsters on their toes,* she would tell the other women of the village, when she bumped into them next and they would agree. Petros steadied himself. He was from a group of young men that were mischievous, always having fun, always smiling but at all times polite, especially to their elders. He would not dream of calling the lady he was working for by her first name, even if he knew it, so called her formally Mrs. or in Greek, Kyria.

"I have to position, on the cill, your geranium pot and its matching terracotta saucer Kyria, with its bright red flowers it is beautiful and you must please leave it where I put it and remember water each morning."

She was not impressed and not for being told what to do.

"You measure to place a pot these days, you youngsters are crazy, too much time on your hands"

Kyria Colos, very old school in her ways, still thought of Petros and his friends as schoolchildren as, there being only three years between the oldest and youngest in the group, they had all attended the same class and she had sometimes helped out in school if the teacher was ill, all that time ago.

"It is not like our winter village when we are down here in Skala" Petros continued. "Our summer home by the sea is now for tourists as well as us. You have lovely whitewashed walls, beautiful blue shutters thanks to me, and now, the geraniums must be one third the way across the window cill for balance. Not in the middle. Believe me Kyria, tourists will explore these back streets away from the harbour, they will believe that they alone have discovered your window, they will take lots of photos of your shutters and show their friends back home and then more tourists will come and we will all be rich!"

Petros had made a chalk mark on the third and descended the ladder to get the geranium and laughed to himself at the tirade coming from the window about having agreed a price to paint the shutters and no extra costs for chalk marks and lifting geraniums onto window cills. Neither Petros nor Kyria Colos were aware of the ancient traditions that they employed with house and shutter colours. It was natural to all those in the village to pastel colour their house walls and pick out highlights in blue – it gave the village a harmony with, not only the surrounding sun-bleached land but with the myriad shades of blue of the sea and sky also.

The annual cycle was continuing as it had done in his father's youth. Petros and his friends made money here and money there. Some mending of houses, some house painting. Getting the summer village ready for tourists, keeping the village going through the busy summer months, some work in tavernas when times were very busy, a little fishing here and there for food and for profit, helping with livestock. Later in the year there would be a need for all of them to pick grapes in their own and in the many tiny vineyards dotted around the island and, for some of the boys who had experience, some work in the co-operative winery after the picking. Then the hard times through winter up in the winter village, not hard because of the weather, which was pleasant enough, but because of the lack of work, the lack of money, until it all started again in spring.

Petros was half way back up the ladder, balancing himself while carrying the heavy pot when his mobile rang in his back jeans pocket and he chose to ignore it. His phone had an old ring that made people smile with nostalgia. It was a simple tune from an early mobile. Some of the boys had smart phones now but Petros had always argued for a phone that was just a phone.

The pot was in position and Petros took out his phone and called the last number in his list of missed calls, which belonged to Dimitri.

'Hi, couldn't answer, I am up a ladder looking through a window into the bedroom of Kyria Colos. How about you?'

Jokes were exchanged about Petros needing a girlfriend younger than this new found love in his life and it was then arranged that some of the boys would go to the beach at four that afternoon, after their work. Not enough of them could make it, Petros was told, for a game of football but enough to sit around, have a chat and discuss where the next work was coming from.

Petros returned to his parent's home, carefully negotiating the ladder down narrow streets, placed the communal ladder on two hooks on the back wall of the house and made a mental note to tell the others where 'the ladder' was when he met them later. He was still in sunglasses and sat in his parent's courtyard with the sun on him, the smells of his mother's cooking wafted from the house, clearing the paint smell from his nose and a feeling of contentment gently washed over him.

The boys had, a long time ago, all made a pact before leaving for their national service, that their group would be as tight when they returned as it was when they left. Different ages and different postings meant a five or six year period of splintering and then a re-forming of the bond that grew as strong, if not stronger, than it was before. When in their twenties, each talked of Australia and America and the money to be made there Then one evening, after more than a few beers, Dimitri had said to an assembled group of twelve;

"I see it differently. I think you all look at wages abroad and imagine saving up money and coming back to our island, rich. Who do you know who left and came back? I tell you friends that to live abroad costs all the money that you earn and to get more money will suck the happiness out of you. I will wish you all good luck in your ventures. When you leave there will be less strong men to share the work and I will be busy and happy. But, I will work when I want to work, I will have fifteen different jobs and not one boring or monotonous job and I will come to the beach in the summer afternoons and know that I have been smiling for most of the day."

Amazingly eight of the twelve lads stayed on the island with Dimitri's speech locked into their memories forever. Some had married women from their own and other villages but the island

122

was small enough to keep them all close. Each wife knew the importance of the group to each of the boys and compensated in their demands of their men.

Petros stood, entered the dark and cool rooms of the small house that one day would be his, took off his sunglasses, kissed his mother, respectfully, on the top of her head, asked what time she wanted him back for the evening meal and walked to the beach, to his friends. It was a very familiar walk, he knew every inch of the beach and his friends were each predictable in their character – so why would Petros ever expect that he was walking into a changed future, an hour that would drastically change the rest of his life?

Chapter 8

Rebecca woke early and was lying in bed thinking of a strategy to employ to be able to include her friend in her investigations but keep her out of danger and stop her from making any mistakes that might put them both in danger. Before going down to breakfast in their hotel she revealed to Paraskevi the plan and wondered whether, if they had been still back at her villa, would they each be making their own breakfasts, the boss to housekeeper relationship having seemingly evaporated. She had been teaching Para to seize more power in her life and it seemed to be working.

"I think," Rebecca started "that we should split up duties for part of each day. Today if we go to the taverna on beach one, I will show you how my listening gear works then, later, you can go down on the beach to relax and sunbathe and I will stay listening. If nothing happens we will do the same tomorrow on beach two and carry on to beach three the next day. People tend to stay on the same beach so we should cover all tourists. If anything crops up in Greek I will ask you to sit close by to the people and listen to their conversation. What do you think? Oh, and on one day you can do the round the island tour, they always take in the winery, where you must look and listen without being obvious."

By the time that they managed to get to the dining room, breakfast, usually no big deal anyway on small Greek islands, had finished but there was still some dry cake and coffee left so they helped themselves. When they left their hotel they were equipped with touristy beach bags and walking poles and they left for beach number one. To leave the village by any route would have to be uphill and they walked in silence, both women out of shape, puffing and trying to move that early morning, thickened blood around their bodies. As they left the boundaries of the village Rebecca became acutely aware of the distinct changes in the environment around her. The now distant babbling of village conversation, which in Greece could sometimes sound like arguing, changed to a deafening cacophony of chirping as the cicadas battled with each other for audible supremacy, which to them equalled sexual supremacy. The light, which in the village had been partly shaded by buildings and vine clad pergolas was now reflecting off all the surfaces that it had, over millennia, parched of colour, everything now being one of many shades of light brown. The complicated village aroma, made up of differing proportions of olive oil, tobacco, stifado or rabbit stew being cooked all day in paprika, the aniseed of ouzo and other pungent aromas that she

125

couldn't always quite make out, slowly disappeared. Further down the road, where they had to turn off and start climbing even more steeply, the breeze was coming in over the bay. This pleasant westerly breeze had travelled many miles over the Mediterranean and was salt white and pure, a blotting paper for aromas. Blowing gently through the pinewood in front of them the breeze had picked up the smells of the pine needles, bark and resin. This gentle waft, left the woodland and travelled down the small sub valley, hit Rebecca square in the nostrils, reminded her of retsina wine and the contrast, she decided, with what has gone before in the village could not have been greater.

On arriving at beach number one, as they would forever call it, Rebecca took in and analysed the scene. As far as she was concerned it was perfect for listening-in to conversations. The beach area was compact and made even more compact by the fact that the taverna owner also owned the beds and umbrellas and had congregated them, mainly, around the taverna area hoping that visitors would come to him all day for their drinks and snacks, as well as any meals.

The taverna was really a timber shack with a timber decking seating area and a timber rail between that area and the beach. Rebecca saw the seat she wanted next to that rail overlooking the beach and occupied it. She knew from experience that the taverna owner would not mind her sitting there all day as long as she ordered occasionally and that he would like the fact that she was visible from the beach and was an advert for the fact that he was open and serving. The first law of owning a taverna, Rebecca had been told by Paraskevi, was to get those first few customers in. These early diners would prove to the world that the taverna was popular, more customers would come and the taverna owner could then relax as perpetual motion kept seats occupied for the rest of the evening.

He hadn't really opened but greeted the women as he passed, said good morning in Greek and seemed to know that Para was Greek as he explained to her, in their common language, that he would be back soon. He had a pad and pen in his hand and took off to charge the early risers for their beds and umbrellas.

"Look and learn" Rebecca sounded like a teacher and knew it and smiled. She had her walking pole stretched across the table pointing out under the timber rail and towards the beach.

"I have already taken the rubber bottom off my walking pole and must remember to put it back on before we leave. Inside the pole is a directional, microphone and camera that are blue-toothed to my phone." She picked up her phone and connected her ear buds to it.

Para looks perplexed "except that is not your phone" she joined in as Rebecca handed her the ear buds.

" No, my phone is in my bag on silent, this looks like a modern smartphone but has no transmission facility but a huge, huge memory for recording sound, video and still pictures. You will see me tap my fingers on the table occasionally pretending to be listening to music that is not there. Here, put the ear buds in."

Paraskevi tentatively placed a bud in each ear and listened to nothing. Rebecca switched the unit on, told Para it was not traceable by other phones searching for a blue-tooth partner and started moving the walking pole slightly.

Para grabbed at the pole and Bec's hand in an attempt to stop any further movement. She had a look of shock on her face as she tried to look down the length of the pole to see who was in its path. About eighty yards away a young couple were discussing the couple in the hotel room next to theirs and whether they wanted to go out for a meal with them or not as she was nice but he was a bragging bore. Para listened to every word clearly, as if she was sat next to them. With mouth open, in a state of semi mock shock, she took the ear buds out of her ears and said to Rebecca "You are a very nosey, very naughty woman Rebecca" and then laughed.

Bec carried on scouring the beach and the taverna owner returned and said something very quickly to them in Greek. When Para started to translate for Bec, the taverna owner realised they were not both Greek, apologised and switched to English that sounded as if it had been learnt on the island rather than America or Australia.

"I do coffee straight away, breakfast will take longer."

They both ordered coffee and, to Para's surprise, Bec ordered a cooked breakfast for later on. She'd seen it on the menu and knew that it had been put on there especially for tourists from Northern Europe, there being nothing Greek about bacon, sausage and egg. It was just too tempting for someone who was getting fed up with coffee and dry cake.

"But we had breakfast" Para giggled after the owner had left them. Rebecca explained the difference in cultures. In Greece, especially on the islands, breakfast was literally breaking of a fast with something light, perhaps a piece of cake with a coffee or one ham roll on its own, or, if you were lucky, a saucer of yoghurt and honey. In Britain it could be the main meal that took you through the day, perhaps with a light lunch, and then the evening meal was taken much earlier than in Greece.

"I don't think I can watch you eat fried food so early in the day, I am off for a swim and to lay under an umbrella to enjoy the fact that I am not cooking or serving or even thinking about serving."

After a pretty boring morning, lunchtime arrived and the two women were sat at Rebecca's table contemplating what to eat. Para was finding it too hot on the beach and fancied sitting in the shade for a couple of hours until things cooled down a bit. There was not a lot to talk about as Para had only heard a couple of Greek voices, shouting to each other on the beach and Bec had scanned the whole beach and had nothing to offer other than general chit chat and some conversation in what she thought may be Norwegian or Finnish, it being a bit like German only softer. They both had a beer with their lunch and spent a fair bit of money, allowing Bec to sit for the rest of the afternoon without drinking more coffee as she was in danger of sitting awake all night if she drank any more. They discussed what would happen the following day at beach number two but Para had another idea and called over the taverna owner.

"I have visited your island a number of times as the bones of my mother's grandfather are in a family crypt up by the bone house in the cemetery, but I have never been around the island or learnt anything about the island. Is there a guided tour?"

Not so amazingly for a small island he had a friend with a mini bus that did tours three times a week if he could fill the bus. He rang his friend and there was a trip leaving the port the following day but the tour would be in English. Para explained that this was ok and might improve her English and asked where the tour went to so the taverna owner just handed his mobile to Para and casually wandered off to clear tables and take orders.

"We start at the port and go up the coast to see caves and a beautiful bay and then head inland to a ceramic factory. Here you can look and see how the pots are made and maybe buy something. Then we head to the winery where there is a free tasting and a tour where they explain the wine making process and, of course, if you like the wine, then you can buy some. At the winery there is a small taverna next door where we have a set lunch that is in with the price of the trip and then we head to a rocky bay on the East coast where I will snorkel and pick some spiny urchins which we will cut open and eat with a little lemon juice. Finally we return to the port and visit a jewellery shop where you can watch the goldsmith at work and again you can buy if you wish."

Paraskevi booked the trip and arranged to pay for it in cash the following day. She explained where she was staying and the tour operator told her that he was passing through her adopted village on his way to the port and would pick her up on his way through.

Rebecca gave Para some idea of what she should be looking out for at the winery and resigned herself to a day alone on beach number two, just when she was getting used to having company. At three-thirty Para decided it was cool enough to go back to her beach spot to enjoy the late afternoon and evening warmth but felt a bit resigned to the fact that Bec was on a wild goose chase and that a holiday is what she had achieved but without the hoped for excitement.

Para's bed and umbrella were quite close to the sea with a view of all those that entered the water and she found it intrusive when a group of boys arrived and camped out just in front of her on towels thrown onto the sand. There were four of them, Greek, possibly on holiday and in high spirits. The four boys swam and played like small boys in a childish manner and Para tried to ignore them but couldn't. As they came out of the sea and back to their towels to dry, Para studied them from behind sunglasses as each lay out on the sand. Bec had homed in on them with her walking pole and was listening to quick Greek and

132

understood a conversation that two of them were
having which seemed to be a conversation about
her friend in such a voice that Para too was bound
to be able to hear.

"I tell you she is Greek, nobody outside Greece
could have such a beautiful appearance as that."
this from a lad with wet black hair that almost
reached his muscular shoulders.

"Well I don't recognise her so if she is Greek
then she is from another island. Your parents
would be happy for you to marry a rich Greek
woman from another island who can afford to
come here on holiday, Petros".

They were waiting for a reaction from Para. Did
she understand their quick Greek? She was not
reacting so Petros turned to his friend Avriano and
tried harder.

"I agree with you Avriano when you say it is a
lovely bikini but I think the top is loose and will
come off, perhaps after I have taken the young
lady out for a meal tonight."

This time there was a reaction. Para's mouth
was wide open with shock, perhaps overstated
mock shock, while Petros' face had gone a shade
of red as he wondered if he had gone too far.
Rebecca by this time was giggling, having

understood enough of the Greek conversation to see the funny side of it.

Perhaps Petros should have left things there but he approached Para and spoke to her slowly and quietly, while kneeling beside her in apologetic fashion.

"My dear lady I am so sorry, as you can see I am very embarrassed. Although I argued that you were Greek I believed that you were not and was larking about with my friends and I have been very childish. Please tell me how I can make it up to you".

Rebecca was hooked. She knew she shouldn't be listening to her friend's private conversation but...

"I can think of only one way to make amends for such rudeness" started Para in a very annoyed voice "the meal that you just promised me but with also your solemn promise that whatever top I wear will stay on and that we will be like friends, perhaps to know each other but as friends only."

Rebecca was almost clapping but at the same time hoping that Petros was nothing like Shit-head, but then, how could she judge all the men of a nation based on her experience of one man. The date was arranged for the following night, the boys went off giggling, Petros no doubt being teased about continually looking back over his shoulder to where Para was still on her sun lounger, purposely not watching them go, feigning disinterest. She eventually had enough of sun bathing for the day and, anyway, couldn't contain herself and the women agreed it was time to go and started the walk back to the village to choose clothes for Para's big night out tomorrow after her round the island trip.

Para was talking with excitement about her date with what she saw as the most handsome man on the island if not the whole of Greece. A phrase she used more than once.

"But, he believes that I am a rich enough Greek that I can afford to pay for a holiday on his island"

"Then we mustn't let him think otherwise. It is his own perception, nothing that you have said to him, you are not lying. You and your friend have clubbed together to pay for this holiday. Let him think what he wants until you get to know each other better. Remember, you know nothing about him."

"Bec, I am a bored server in a taverna, he is bound to find out and then it will be all over".

"Look Para, you are jumping way ahead of yourself. (It is an idiom, does not translate into Greek, it means you are looking too far into the

135

future instead of concentrating on the present.) He may well be a bored server in a taverna also. You could be bored together. Anyway, listen; here is where you start looking for the positives in your life. You have described to me your life, you're arguing with your Baba, the dreary side of things. When we look for positives we say that you have a beautiful and successful taverna with sea views on a beautiful island. The taverna is owned by your parents but to go to you and any future husband when they die as you are an only child. Attached to this taverna is a house, across the road from the seating area, which will eventually be accommodation for you and your family with the ground floor already converted to a kitchen area."

"Wow, it sounds lovely, I hardly recognise it. I can't wait to tell my cousin Yiorgo that he is out of the picture."

The rest of the walk back was chit chat about clothes, Rebecca's various perfumes and how to react to any questions that Petros may have. Rebecca was too aware that although she was part of the conversation and was included in the planning of the date, she was clearly not on the date. Friends and lovers she had pushed away or they had left her. Now she was just getting used to being with Para and was jealous of Petros who might take her away. It was an odd feeling to be smiling, to be happy for your friend, to be sad inside

Chapter 9

It was not early when Rebecca managed to slip out of sleep. The sun was already high and heating the hotel room to an unbearable temperature and breakfast would have finished an hour or so ago. The instant coffee in the room had not been replenished, there were no cold drinks or water that could be seen from her viewpoint lying in bed and Paraskevi's single bed was empty as she had been picked up earlier by the tour driver in his mini-bus. Rebecca felt depressed and very alone. Her mood was not improved while showering and dressing. She knew this feeling and hated it. The soap kept slipping from her hand, landing with a thud on the shower tray, shampoo got in her eye when she bent over to retrieve the soap, the towel wrapped around her fell to the ground, twice, and then the shorts she was going to wear could not be found. Life was saying to her "Sometimes everything goes right, sometimes it all goes wrong. Today is a day where it will all go wrong and perhaps you should stay in bed."

Leaving the hotel she started walking in the direction of beach number two and knew just about enough of the layout of the village to be confident that she had seen a café on her route, that she would reach before hitting the village boundary. The first thing that day seemed to go right as Bec found the café taverna where she expected it to be. There was movement within so she sat at a table under a pergola that was holding up an ancient grape vine, the leaves of which, she reasoned might cut down the light and heat. A young woman served her, reminding her of Para except that this woman had no English. The conversation they had in Greek, well, broken tourist Greek, revealed the fact that the taverna was not yet open for business, they were preparing for lunch, that the woman had just made herself an instant coffee and would make one for Rebecca without charge. Yes, it was going to be one of those days.

The coffee didn't take long to make or to drink and, in the short time she had, Rebecca consulted her map to prove to herself that she was going in the right direction. Getting lost now would really round things off for her. There was a huge contrast between today and yesterday that was affecting her mood, a mood that was by no means a clinical depression but felt like it at that moment. Yesterday had seemed free and easy as she'd wandered out of the village with Para, almost as if it didn't matter if they had gone the wrong way. Today she was back to the regimented Rebecca, precise, working efficiently. At that very moment she preferred yesterday, preferred the ease of the day and preferred company to solitude. Then, a realisation, if Para returned from her round the island tour and changed to get picked up for her date while Bec was out, then they wouldn't see each other until later that night and this depressed Bec even more, a feeling she was slowly getting used to.

With a bottle of water purchased from a supermarket Rebecca hiked through the heat, the sun getting stronger as it was approaching midday. There was no sound of cicadas, there was no breeze with the scent of pine, in fact there was no breeze full stop. The beach was below a small car abandoning area, too unorganised to be called a car park, the path then leading down a steep slope where there was a small shop but no taverna. There was a high, flat, rocky area above the beach that Rebecca immediately realised would be her vantage point, although it would only cover half of the beach.

Rebecca laid out her towel on a long, flat rock, placed her mini rucksack at one end for a pillow, placed her walking stick along the length of the towel for later and abandoned it all to investigate the shop, returning with a crusty roll of margarine and processed ham. This being her first food of the day, Bec decided that today would be one of her diet days, as she didn't really have a choice. The roll was supplemented by two small overpriced bottles of water and a packet of gum, thrust at her instead of the coins that the shopkeeper didn't have, to be able to give her change. As the crusty roll was consumed, just about leaving Bec's teeth still in her mouth, she contemplated whether to use her listening device or whether to just relax for the day and do nothing, so that nothing else could go wrong. Her mood was such that she thought that she may well tell Para tonight that it was all a wild goose chase and they were going back to their own island. Was she feeling down enough to even go back to her large holiday hotel and watch anorexics tying their hair up, she wondered? In a brief moment of deep depression she realised that she was sat on a beach, on her own while paying her friend two hundred euros a day to go on a round the island trip and later to have a possible holiday romance.

With ear buds wired into her listening device set-up, Rebecca tried to get back into reality and do some work. Conversations that she picked up were boring but then she eventually picked up on a husband and wife with two children aged about five and eight. She dismissed the idea that came into her mind that she might have been concentrating on a family because she was feeling down, missing not having a husband and kids of her own, and she listened to the two languages being spoken. Eventually she worked the family out. Mum was British, English, Southern England somewhere. She spoke a small amount of French, enough to understand her children's conversation with their father but Dad was very French, possibly from the south-west and definitely not from Paris. Dad conversed with the children in French, Mum talked to them in English. Both children could speak both languages fluently and switched from one to the other, seamlessly and, apparently, without thinking about it. Dad's English was much better than Mums French so the couple conversed with each other in English.

Mum kept moving her head while talking, organising things, looking for items that the boys demanded of her and Bec was picking up only bits of her side of the conversation. She could tell that Mum was anxious about something and Dad was making light of it. Bec's brain kick started when she thought she heard Mum say 'wine boxes' but couldn't be certain that she heard correctly. For the next hour the conversation reverted to mundane matters about the kids and about Mum's wish for the kids to attend the English School in Paris if only they could afford the fees. Dad told her the two things were linked. Could this be a link between lots of money and a wine box? Was Rebecca on one of her super exaggeration trips, desperate for something to click into place?

In the late afternoon she made a mental note to return to the same beach the following day to hopefully listen to some more from the family. The rest of the beach conversations were dead.

The shop did not hold enough for a second meal, even the crusty ham rolls had gone. Bec called it a day, a poor day by any standards. At least the sun had started to go down and the heat was less intense as she shuffled slowly back towards the village and her hotel.

On entering the hotel room, Rebecca was half expecting, half hoping, that Para would still be there, full of conversation about her day-trip and excited about her upcoming date. Instead Bec was greeted by the scene that was probably similar to how it would have looked had they been robbed. Most of her dresses and other clothes were spread over both single beds and a very strong smell of mixed perfumes filled the air. Para had been and gone and left a trail of devastation behind her. Bec threw her rucksack, from the door to a corner next to her bed, turned around and walked out of the hotel without showering or changing and headed to the taverna where she had drunk a coffee that morning. When she started eating she realised how hungry she actually was and decided to have wine with her meal. What was that about a diet day again? Maybe tomorrow? She needed to relax before returning to the hotel to hang up all her clothes so that they would not get ruined when an inebriated Para arrived home. She would also have to practice a false smile for when Para excitedly talked about her day and her date, above all though she had to get out of the, now uncomfortable, bikini under her dress.

Sat down, back in the hotel on the end of her bed, she was full of food, too much food. The dresses were away in the wardrobe, possibly even on the side allocated to them when they'd first arrived. Bec was weary. Weary from the sun, weary from the walking, weary from too much food and the carafe of wine but, most of all weary of craving company. In desperation, she sent a text to Paraskevi. She was knowingly intruding but wanted to wish her well and ask her how things were going. No text came back, no Para came home that night and so Bec climbed into bed and very quickly nodded off.

Chapter 10

Petros drifted slowly out of sleep but still had closed eyes, feeling unusually lethargic, full of last night's meal and wondering whether, after his always-at-the-same-time early morning poo, he could manage to go for a short run to wake his body up. It wouldn't be a long 'around the island' run, nor a hard 'up the mountain' run, just a 'maybe run and see where you end up' type run. He started to turn his body very slowly, to get on his back but stay within the single sheet covering him. His eyes started to open, looking for the clock that should be on his bed-side table. Instead he found himself puzzling over the beam in the ceiling, with a goat bell hanging from it, neither of which should have been there. Before he could turn the full ninety degrees, he bumped into Paraskevi's warm and smooth body and the reality of last night's dreamlike date came flooding back into his brain.

Para was already extremely awake, was sat up in bed and spoke first.

"Morning, you look groggy, are you a night owl because I, my friend, am a morning lark"

"Ah, Paraskevi, my Girl Friday, the morning lark makes the coffee in this house" was Petros' quick reply as all thought of going for a run evaporated.

Para jumped out of bed and as she walked to the small kitchen off the bedroom area told Petros, without looking back at him "I am nobody's Girl Friday, even though Friday is what my name means, I am, nobody's slave, but you look incapable so I will make the coffee this time."

As she added 'this time' she cringed inwardly to think she may have gone too far by assuming a next time.

"Good" Petros brain was starting to work and he had now lifted himself onto one elbow "because I am no Robinson Crusoe" but then, added almost to himself "although I feel like it on my little island sometimes."

Para had her back to him and was aware that she could be seen from the bed and that Petros was probably studying her body in bra and pants, the bra that he promised to leave on and had faithfully kept his promise. How glad she was now that she had borrowed Rebecca's classy underwear, found still in its plastic wrapping. The matches were next to the stove that was connected by a dangerously old rubber pipe, to a large gas bottle and she had the stove lit in no time. Opening the top cupboard she found the instant coffee and two mugs, there was some milk in the small fridge and then turning to catch Petros staring at her and smiling to himself like the cat that had the cream, asked him, above the noise of the gas flame,

"Where are the spoons?"

"I guess they are probably in the old drawer unit opposite the sink"

"You don't know?"

"No, this is the house of Nicholias, he stayed with Dimitri last night, I live with Mama and Baba. I thought I told you I was only eight years old."

Coffee making was abandoned, the stove turned off. Para returned slowly and sat on the end of the bed, grabbed the sheet that they'd shared last night and pulled it up to cover the front of her body.

"So it was expected that I would sleep with you on our first date and you boys planned it all together and the whole island thinks how easy I am?"

"No, nothing like that, you have jumped to too many conclusions."

Petros made to grab Para and pull her towards him but failed as she pulled back out of his reach, pulling the sheet off Petros in his underpants, making him feel even more vulnerable than he already felt in his explanation.

"Listen carefully, I will explain. Firstly we did not sleep with each other last night. Well, we slept in the same bed but you know what I mean. I am not the sort to boast of a conquest that did not happen so calm down. Nicholias and Dimitri were both doing night work last night, guarding the winery and, when you went to the toilet in the taverna I rang Nicholias and explained the situation and asked him if he could, after his shift, go to Dimitri's house to sleep for a few hours, instead of coming back here. It was either that or I ruined a wonderful evening by taking you back to your hotel and saying good night and then walking home alone to the house of my parents to lay awake all night thinking about you."

Para was still half annoyed but also thrilled to think that Petros would think that he could lay in bed all night thinking about her, as she would have done the same.

"You are half off my fishing hook but not entirely free yet. Tell me about where you live. You listened to me all last night because you couldn't get a word in – probably my nerves, I don't always go on and on like that, I promise. Well maybe I do, maybe I am now. Do you really live with your parents? What do you do to earn money? I want to know all about you because I am nosey but also because you now owe it to me"

Petros sighed. In his opinion his was a simple life that was made simple by complications. Did that make sense? Could he explain it to Para?

"Okay, are you ready for all this? Yes, I live with my parents, many unmarried men on the island do and you told me last night that you too live with yours. There are eight of us in our little band of brothers but you only saw four of us on the beach. Did I tell you that last night? I can't remember. We each do anything we can for money and share the work out so everyone has equal amounts of work and money. If one of us has a long term job, and by long term I mean about a month, then we can get bored quite quickly and we will swap jobs with someone else in the group. It is not a problem; the other people on the island are aware of how it all works and accept it."

Para grunted like a Greek wife keeping reins on a husband and said "go on, I am still listening" and returned to the kitchen, found the spoons and carried on making coffee but this time with the bed sheet wrapped around her and tied in a knot over her chest. Striking up the gas stove again she spoke louder over the hissing "So, you do all your little jobs for cash then"?

149

"I know what you are thinking, Greece is down the toilet pan because nobody pays their taxes but I do on some of the money, just not all. I will explain with an example. Yesterday I painted a shutter for a local lady. We haggled over a price. I said twenty-five, she said ten and we settled on fifteen which was, to be honest, a fair price. If she had said no at that price then none of my friends would have undercut me and, believe me, they would have all known about my bottom price within an hour of me being refused. Was I supposed to send five of my fifteen to Athens to keep the government offices going? My fifteen paid for a beautiful meal with a beautiful lady and, before you ask, I did have enough money on me to pay for both meals before you insisted on paying for yourself. Let's face it Para, you have a taverna with a very high amount of cash flowing through it. Do you pay every bit of tax"?

Para didn't answer the question but returned to the bed and put Petros' coffee on the small table next to him, sat on his side of the bed, purposely within his arms reach but still had the sheet around her. "This is about you, not me. So the little you earn keeps you going through the year?"

Petros was serious in his explanation and didn't yet reach out to hold her near.

"Yes, some years are better than others of course. We have different lifestyles you and me.

150

Say we both went to the beach with our fifteen euros yesterday. You paid for two beds, even though there is only one of you, an umbrella, a bottle of water and who knows what else. I arrived with my towel and placed it on the beach, had an old plastic bottle of water filled from the tap of my parent's house with fresh spring water that was fresher than your water and I still had my fifteen euros when we left the beach."

Para was amused to think that Petros believed her lifestyle was glamorous and that he didn't realise that, if it wasn't for the pay of Rebecca she too would have been on a towel on the sand.

"So, do you pay any tax? I know that when I paid for my umbrella and beds I gave the man my money and told him that I thought he had already given me a receipt but it had blown away in the wind. He understood, of course, pocketed the cash and seemed grateful."

"We pay some tax but it is complicated. You know already that we all share our jobs and this includes us all taking it in turns to guard the winery from thieves. There is a lot of computer equipment and valuable stainless steel in there and it needs guarding. Two of the boys have a permanent night job doing that work and because the winery came from EU money, everything must be transparent and documented so the boys are paid each week with pay slips that show that their

151

taxes have been taken out. So they get bored of the work, or they suddenly have some day work, or they just want to share the work about, so they swap with one of the other six. In truth, we all do about the same amount of hours doing the guarding. So, two boys are paid in cash, after tax and they then have to pay the other boys who have worked there, in cash. Obviously they have to pay them their hourly rate after the tax has come out or they themselves would be losing out. So eight boys have all paid the tax on the two pay slips and everyone is happy, including the government who, let's face it don't care as long as they get their money."

Para was fascinated by this simple life with all its complications but wanted to know more. Not about the winery and it's guarding, she would tell Rebecca about that, and her visit to the winery, later. No, at the moment she was more fascinated by Petros, how open he was how respectful he had turned out to be and how thin his waist was even though he had wide shoulders as he looked up from his lower position on the bed balanced on one elbow with the coffee mug in the other hand. The sight of his waist and shoulders had not escaped her when they had first met on the beach but now she was observing more intently. His skin was dark, even for a Greek. It was not the darkness of the fake tan of a new tourist and not the darkness of a sunbathed tourist or rich sunbathed Greek from Athens, but the darkness of a manual worker who had sweated in the sun and had been forced to work, shirtless, and, of course, play football on the beach, wearing trunks.

"I am sorry; I have pinched the whole sheet." She suddenly realised this but did nothing to rectify the situation, deciding instead to carry on enjoying the view. "You complained earlier that you sometimes feel like Robinson Crusoe on your small island. Explain to me what you meant because I feel like that too sometimes on my island – coming here is a holiday for my brain as well as my body".

As Petros explained, Para half listened and half thought about how different Petros was to all the other men that she knew. On her island she knew every man in her own age group that lived there, their job, their cousins and their moods. She had grown up with most of them and attended school with a lot of them. Petros was like nothing she had come across before, full of a passion for life and a growing passion for her, hopefully. Perhaps the fact that he was so different was his fascination to her or perhaps it was that, for the first time in her life, it felt like someone was putting her in front of their own selfish feelings. She needed to get to know him better and even maybe concentrate on what he had been saying to her.

"Oh, it wasn't a complaint, the Robinson Crusoe thing. I run. I run sometimes on the flat around the island's coast roads. Sometimes straight up the mountain that you can see in the middle of our island and, once a year, in Athens which is the only time I leave the island, and often the only time I can afford to leave the island."

Para was astonished but understood now that the thin waist was not from a lack of food. "Athens?" was her one word, astonished, comment.

"My running on this island is partly for fun and enjoyment, partly to keep fit and partly for training for the Athens Marathon once a year. If you yourself don't run then you might not know that this marathon starts in the town of Marathon, on the coast. This is the town that all other marathons throughout the world are named after. Runners from all over the world come to Marathon and run the first thirty two kilometres uphill, through little villages, until we reach the outskirts of Athens where it becomes flatter for the last ten kilometres. The highlight is to run into the horseshoe shaped Panathanaikos Stadium arena to finish, feeling like a gladiator or a Greek god. The stadium is only a hundred odd years old but made entirely of marble. I often cry on that last lap, being cheered like a hero by my countrymen."

Para's mouth was open wide; she missed all the detail at the end and just said, in the voice of an unbelieving statement "You run forty two kilometres in one go."

"Yes, it is a lovely feeling when the pain stops as they say. If you hadn't been beside me this morning and I had been at home with my kit, I would have gone for a run into the countryside and perhaps stopped to listen to a nightingale singing just before dawn. I am fascinated by these things. I need to know what birds, trees, animals, plants are around me. Their names and what they do. I cannot just take life, and the things around me, for granted, like most people do".

Para had a contribution to the conversation that didn't involve running and where she thought she might be able to join in with this strange world that was being described to her.

"Ah yes, so easy to find out these things these days with a search engine on your phone."

"No, no, no." Petros raised his hands to face Para, feigned mock horror in his face "This is the biggest argument I have with my friends. Look at this ancient phone. It does what it says it should do. It phones. My friends see a nightingale, if they can be bothered they search on their phones and learn about a nightingale - and then it is gone. I see a nightingale; I buy an old fashioned paper book

155

about Greek birds. It is not gone. I learn about other birds. Para, do you know that we islanders take a bird called the Eleanor's Falcon for granted because they are common here and breed everywhere throughout our islands. We destroy their nest sights to erect more and more buildings next to the sea. What we don't appreciate is that sixty seven percent of these birds that live in Madagascar off the coast of Africa, come back to our islands to breed. If we got rid of them or their nesting sights on our islands we would practically wipe out two thirds of the entire world population."

Para was impressed. Not interested in the slightest with the fate of Eleanor's whatsit but, none the less she was impressed with his passion for nature and for running. This talk of phones also reminded her how useless her own smart phone was, now that it had no battery power and how she should have rung Rebecca before it eventually died. Of course she'd had other things on her mind.

"Petros, I don't know what you are looking for in life but have a good idea of your passions. I will have to be frank and honest with you as I do not have long on your island and if you disagree with me or think I am too forward then please let me know, tell me what you think truthfully before I get too serious after just one date. I like you very

156

much and do not want this to be a one date affair and I don't think you do either. Neither do I want it to be a holiday romance where we rush everything into the two weeks we have together and then never see each other again. I would like to take it slowly, get to know each other more and, if things progress, meet each other again after my holiday, on your island or on my island. I told you all about my situation last night, about Yiorgo and the taverna and all that. I don't want that life but I don't know what life I do want." And then suddenly she added "Oh shit, I'm coming on too strong and too clingy after one meal together, aren't I?"

Petros laughed out loud. "You have summed up how I feel about you, exactly. We are both old fashioned Greeks and life is too short." And then threw in a joke "I will marry you tomorrow in the local church and come to your island and kick Yiorgo out and run your parent's taverna with you but on one condition, that you make another coffee and, this time, take that ridiculous sheet off. I cannot see through it to the beauty that I was studying earlier. I know your bra and pants cover the same amount of flesh as your bikini but somehow you look a lot sexier now."

Paraskevi ran to the kitchen, giggling and leaving the sheet on the bed. "I am in no hurry to go today. My friend will be on a beach somewhere on

her own by now and I won't see her until tonight. I
need to go back to the hotel to find my charger
and charge this damn phone though. What did
you have planned for today?"

Chapter 11

Rebecca's early morning walk back to beach number two was well prepared and more comfortable than the day before and so it felt shorter and quicker. She had provisioned herself with food and drink by filling her other, larger, rucksack and walked with more of a spring in her step. Admittedly, Paraskevi was still on her mind, especially the fact that she had not rung and not answered any texts or voice messages but she tried hard to get that out of her mind and felt as if she could concentrate more on the French come English family, just in case there was something to concentrate on. Today she was wearing a loose and light, red dress, showing her change in mood. The dress was over a black bikini, the white of yesterday making her skin both look, and feel pale. On her head a large brimmed, straw hat for the practical reason of keeping the sun off her head but with a disguise factor thrown in. Her large sunglasses, that almost covered her face, instead of the small pair of yesterday, accompanied by bright red lipstick, changed her appearance completely. Smiling as she walked, it was going to be a much better, more organised day than yesterday, even down to the detail of having, in her rucksack a towel that nobody on the island had yet seen. The only giveaway, to

anyone on beach number two, to the fact that she
was the same woman as yesterday, would be the
fact that she walked with a walking pole – so
today she had it telescoped down and in her
rucksack.

She recognised the bend just before the car
abandoning area above the beach and knew that,
as she rounded the bend, there would be cars
faced in all different directions with no semblance
of there being any organisation of the area. What
she wasn't ready for was the sight of the French
family exiting a tiny, little, Fiat. She immediately
sat on the side of the road on a grassed ridge that
followed the road on both sides and had been
created from the spoil from when the makeshift
gravel road had first been built. The new seat
taking the weight of her rucksack, she loosened
the straps from her arms, calmly took a drink
from her bag and started drinking from the bottle
while feeling the cool of her back as the sweat
evaporated from where the rucksack had been.
The French family went through, what appeared
to be, a daily ritual of trying to get organised for
the day and trying to get the two boys organised
at the same time. It was Dad's job to load himself
up, like a pack-horse, with all the bags that were
needed for the day and, having his bags, he was
on his way. It was Mum's job to organise two
young over-excited boys and to tell everyone
around her that nobody ever listened to her and

she might as well not try to get the boys to the beach and they should all go back to the hotel. Rebecca smiled to hear the older boy listen to his mother's grumbles in English and answer her in her second language, French, to annoy her, to try and get the upper hand over her. Rebecca was, for a moment, transported back to her English and Welsh language youth, her selective hearing and selective choice of language. This mum was now so flustered that she slammed the door of the car and marched off, still shouting at the older boy, while dragging the younger boy by the wrist. She had left without locking the car. No lights had flashed.

Rebecca saw the chance of looking into the car window for any clue, after the family had finally and noisily disappeared from view. With nobody else around, in the sudden silence, she walked calmly to the car and looked in through the front, side windows and, at the same time, bobbed her head up to look over the roof to see if anyone from the family was coming back up from the beach. The usual array of rubbish sat on the car's floor, no doubt to be cleared out on the last day of their holiday, but nothing of interest to Rebecca. She bobbed her head up over the low roof again, still nobody about, time to look in the back seats. There, in front of her, in the well of the back seat was a bag, the zipped top of which was open. Rebecca opened the door very slowly in case it was alarmed, as if opening it slowly would make any difference to whether the alarm activated or not. She knew that if the alarm sounded then she would have to close the door quickly and walk away and let people think that the alarm had gone off because of heat, or a fly or some other weird thing that made alarms go off for no apparent reason. The alarm did not go off.

She rummaged through the bag quickly and found a letter, presumably addressed to the wife in Saint-Emilion, a town that she knew well and, for a second, she had to force herself to concentrate on the task at hand and push out of her mind the memories that came flooding into her mind. James, the love of her life, at that time in her youth, had convinced her to hitch hike through France and they had spent happy weeks picking grapes in the Saint-Emilion region. The bag was full of the usual rubbish but no paperwork or anything else tying the family into any wrong doing and then she came across, at the bottom of the bag, a car key. A spare for this Fiat? No, it had a Peugeot symbol on it, was not the flick knife type of key and had no buttons or battery so yes, possibly a spare to an older Peugeot, a key that would obviously not fit this Fiat. A loose piece of yellow coloured electrical wire ran through the ring at the top of the key, holding a card label, on it written "Omereau, we pick you up, floor D bay 32, Kyria Jeune." Not knowing quite why, Rebecca slipped the key into her own bag, took a photograph of the address label on the envelope to the wife of the Jeune family in Saint-Emilion, closed the car door and left for the beach.

The French family were sat in exactly the same spot as yesterday, among yesterday's sand castles and the boys make-believe city - but Rebecca's rock ledge spot at the top of the beach was taken so she moved further along the ledge and settled on what appeared to be a flat bit and, on looking up, she realised that she had a more direct line to the family that she wanted to listen to. She might even, from this angle, be able to catch Mum's speech as her head swung from Dad to the boys and back, as it did yesterday. She organised herself while, occasionally, glancing over to her target family where, Dad had now dropped all his bags and, his work for the day being over, he was playing with the boys while mum was organising towels, emptying bags and generally organising their "patch".

With her striped towel out of her rucksack, the pole with microphone by her side, ear buds into her fake phone and her e-book on the rocky ledge, Rebecca lay on her side as if she was reading the blank e-book screen and appeared to anyone looking to be totally uninterested with anything that happened elsewhere on the beach.

With everything within the family now organised and the boys covered in suntan lotion, it was safe for dad to lie down next to his wife and let the boys re-enter their imaginary, sand castle, world so that he could talk to her seriously.

"It is difficult that we can only talk about it while the boys are playing or asleep but, once again, there is absolutely no risk. Risk only happens when something is unusual at borders and we will be a normal family in our normal car returning, tired, from a normal holiday from Greece, travelling through Italy. We will not be driving through Albania or any other of those awkward countries. Even if everything in the car is searched nothing can be found. The route has been used lots of times without a problem" French Dad was calming English Mum but she was still looking tense and replied,

"I don't like it. I know the risk is low, I know the rewards are great, especially for the boys and school and all that, but I worry, you know I do. What if something does go wrong next week on the ferry or even in Bari, we know France but don't know how things are in Italy?"

French Dad was getting exasperated but still talking quietly and smiling at his boys when they turned towards him "The only thing that can go wrong is with the wine box labels and that is in our hands. The buyers in Paris are trusted, there will be no rip off like you see in films, and they are old customers of the person I spoke to and want to use this route again. It is big money for us Cherie. You'll be happier when we are back in our own car in our own country. You know that I will unload our car of you, the kids and the holiday cases before travelling back up to Paris to make the swap. You and the kids will not be involved".

Rebecca had all this conversation digitally recorded and would listen to it again when she got back to her hotel room, listen to it very carefully and work out what Mum was referring to when Rebecca thought she heard her refer to Barry, the town next to Barry Island where Rebecca and her family spent many a hot weekend day when she was young. The important thing was that she was now totally convinced that wine boxes held the key to what was going on and, what was going on was drug smuggling into France as well as separately into Britain and to 'Shady Character.' If Paraskevi and her Greek rumours were correct then the route was; heroin made from poppies grown in Afghanistan, sent with an Afghan courier as far as Turkey where a people smuggler would take illegal immigrants to Greece, including the courier whose passage was paid for by the Afghan bosses. The heroin was then somehow blended with wine into wine boxes, given, in this case, to an average looking French family, who then somehow get in their Peugeot (*in Athens? Can they drive it if I have the key?*) They then drive to France and meet trusted people who take the wine boxes and hand over cash in payment to the family before breaking down and cutting the powder and sending it through many hands towards people on the street. The irony was not lost on Rebecca that this family was prepared to see the downfall of people, even cause their eventual death, in order to provide a good education and upbringing for, what they saw as, their perfect little family.

All this was going through Rebecca's mind while she listened as the family talked about sand castles, lunch and who hit who first. Then her attention was directed elsewhere. Down onto the beach walked Paraskevi and the man who Rebecca recognised as being Petros. They were gripping onto each other tightly, each one afraid to let the other one go, her holding the back of his shirt near the collar, him holding on to her hip bone with his hand occasionally wandering over the line of her curvy waist, drawing her towards his body so tightly that the pair could not walk in a straight line. Constantly looking into each other's eyes, they giggled and appeared not to notice about fifty other people on the beach and would not have noticed Rebecca if she had jumped out in front of them, singing. Arriving at the edge of the sea they settled, with him doing an impression of a waiter and offering her the towel on the sand, only one towel being needed if they were to stay that close to each other. Stripping down to their bathers made Rebecca whisper out loud "Bitch, she told me she never borrowed my bikinis. What's that then?"

Rebecca made a promise to herself not to listen to any part of their, probably sickening, conversation.

Watching Paraskevi and Petros while listening to mundane English from the French family allowed Bec to, once again, remember the good times in France, with James. They had taken a few jobs before reaching Saint-Emilion and she could remember being in the high topped village, looking out over a vista of vineyards and wondering if they could ever live in such a beautiful place. There was an evening too, when they had money enough to go for a meal, to celebrate something or other, and they had got soaked in a downpour and dried with towels by the restaurant staff. This had meant a lot to Bec because she could remember writing one of her poems and only seemed to write them if something big happened in her life. Where that poem was now was anyone's guess, she certainly couldn't remember the words. What she could remember though was feeling smothered by

James, telling him she was too young to get really serious and him then being with a blonde German grape picker within a couple of hours of their conversation. Rebecca's travel through Europe, following the grape harvest and later the olive harvest, had been a lonely one, lonelier even than she felt now.

The French family had gone completely off the boil with the conversation concerning the worries of Mrs. Jeune obviously closed. Rebecca had some thinking to do especially if this family were going to be in Italy next week on whatever day it would be. It was time to have something to eat and drink before going back to the hotel, plan the next few days out and work out what her next conversation with Paraskevi was going to entail.

The long drag of a walk back to the hotel gave Rebecca time to dwell on things. She would not tell Paraskevi about what she had heard today because it could get Para into trouble and, even worse, if Para mentioned anything to Petros then Rebecca herself could find things getting troublesome. She would tell Para that it was all a wild goose chase, that she shouldn't have been so nosey, that she was probably leaving before the end of their holiday, and that Para could stay on if she wished as the hotel was paid for and Para had her open return ticket on the catamaran back to her island and that Rebecca would contact her when she got back to Cornwall.

Working out how to follow the French family would be trickier. The opportunity to give them their Peugeot key back had disappeared when she passed the car on the road back to her hotel, stopping only to pretend to check her mail on her phone while taking a photograph of the registration plate of the Fiat, her memory incapable of remembering Greek number plates.

Showering when she got back gave her more time to think and meant that she could change straight into cool pyjamas even though it was still early afternoon. Her mobile phone battery was low so she reached out for her backup battery pack to find that it was gone and her charging lead, held to the battery pack with an elastic band, gone with it.

Getting angrier with Para by the minute, she concentrated on the search engine results on her laptop and worked out that most probably;– the family would get a catamaran from this island back to Piraeus, the port of Athens. Probably their car was in a car parking garage there called Omereau and they would be met at the port by the Omereau people, but she would research that at a later date. Looking at Ferry routes on her laptop screen she discovered that a ferry left the west coast of Greece, a car drive away from Athens and it sailed, not to Barry Island in Wales, astonishingly, but to Barri in Italy.

Things were taking shape but Rebecca didn't know when the family were leaving for Italy or how she would follow them to France; two huge questions.

Rebecca placed a bedside table in the middle of the room, placed her camera tripod over it with the three legs on the floor, took the central column out of the top of the tripod and refitted it underneath so that an attached camera could take close-up photos of something on the table and chose a macro, close-up lens to go on her SLR camera. With two mini LED lights, clipped to two of the tripod legs, the strange looking configuration was ready to take detailed, close-up photos of the key.

There was just enough power in her mobile to be able to make a call to someone she knew in France. He was in her contacts list as Pierre De La Clé, or Peter of the key, but she had no idea what his real name was and no real desire to know. She was three quarters of the way through a conversation with Pierre when Para burst into the room, thankfully alone. Para stopped, looked at the camera gear and sat on the end of her bed waiting for Rebecca to finish her conversation which luckily for Rebecca was in French.

"...Yes, I can do that, the file sizes are around 50Mb each so I will place them all in a file on my hosting site and send you a link so that you can download them. The scale rule in the shots is graduated to half millimetres so hopefully accurate enough. So you need both sides and an end on shot. I'll pay the 350 into the account of the e-mail address you gave me before I send the photos. You have my address here in Greece and say it will be with me in a couple of days.

Thanks again, speak to you next time no doubt."

Rebecca would have liked time to try and explain the camera equipment to Para but Para had been patiently awaiting a chance to get into full flow on how she was the happiest woman on the planet. Para jumped in before Bec could open her mouth,

"Bec, it is incredible, he is so sweet, so understanding, so passionate, so handsome, like nothing on my island, do you know he runs up mountains and stops to listen to nightingales, he goes to Athens to run uphill 42 kilometres and he shares all his work with seven of his friends."

Para stopped to breathe in and saw Rebecca's eyes large with amazement. Rebecca knew that, with her own track record, she was far from being the best judge of character when it came to men but what was being described to her here, were not the qualities that she usually looked for.

"Para, I know you are excited and in love but have you thought this through? You live on different islands, or didn't you notice."

Para casually took out the battery back up unit from her bag and placed it on Rebecca's bed, not attempting an apology as she placed it over-carefully and explained.

"My phone died which is why I couldn't contact you to say where I was. I picked this up lunchtime, I knew you wouldn't mind. I have more apologies too. I told you I never borrowed underwear or bikinis, which is true, but when I knew I was going out with him and looked at my bras and horrible bikini, well, not inspiring. Don't take this the wrong way but I think my boobs are pretty good and with my boobs in your bra, well, it had him panting like a dog, like a fish on my line, he even joked about marrying me and coming to my island to run the taverna. One more thing and I hope I did right, you have told me how you are off men and you have told me about your experience with a Greek man, so when Petros suggested two couples go for a meal I said you were not available. Was this ok? I worried that you could have had fun or a romance and maybe I spoiled it because I just wanted to be with Petros and nobody else around."

Rebecca had calmed down about everything that she thought she was angry about and was just pleased for Para and her young love.

"I am happy for you and your hill running bird watcher and hope all goes well but I am afraid my nosiness has come to a dead end. It won't be immediately but I think I will be going back to my villa some time soon. This hotel is paid for until the end of our holiday and you have your return catamaran ticket and I am guessing you want as much time with Petros as possible so will stay here?"

Para waited, head down, thinking through her next bit of conversation, how she would say things without hurting Rebecca.

"Bec, I have worked for you on this island up until this morning so you should not pay me after that. To be honest, if it is a choice between the work you want me to do with all its money, compared with spending time with Petros when he is not working, then there is no choice for me. I have never believed this nosey- lady thing but didn't know whether you were British police or Greek police, either way this camera equipment confirms my thoughts. Anyway, without trying to insult you, if you think the winery is a dead end then you are not very good at your job, I think."

Rebecca was a bit taken aback. How much did Para know? Her eyes were raised again as she waited for Para to continue.

"I have not discussed any of this with Petros, I don't want him involved. Petros and his seven mates take it in turns to guard the winery overnight to safeguard computer equipment and the stainless steel tanks. Number one, the computer equipment is a ten year old PC with a very deep screen, you remember these? Of course the information on the computer could be the valuable bit, so make a copy every night, job done. Number two. The stainless steel that is so valuable is in the huge wine vats. Nobody on this island would spill the wine to get at the valuable metal, they all own the wine. Who is going to come to the island, from outside, and spill out all the wine and spend hours cutting up the vats into pieces small enough to carry and then get the pieces off the island without anyone seeing? None of it makes sense. My visit to the winery, before I found out about the guarding, was interesting. Here is the sales leaflet for wines, it has no wine boxes available. I explained about my taverna on my island and the lady gave me a trade price list, again no wine boxes. The camera you gave me and told me to take lots of photos, I kept it strapped around my neck and kept pressing the button, only lifting it to my eye a couple of times when something was interesting to tourists, basically when other people took photos. Here is the camera. This either confirms all your suspicions or makes you feel there is no more to look at here. All I ask of you, my friend is that if there is trouble coming that you let me know to get Petros away from the trouble. In return I promise not to mention our conversations to anyone. Petros is working now but I will meet him later for a meal and will probably not be back tonight."

Rebecca gratefully received the camera and all the information from Para, who showered, changed in the bathroom and left to meet the love of her life. Rebecca felt she owed Para a bit of an explanation and anything she could do to help her relationship with Petros. From feeling angry at Para she now felt the reverse and wanted to help as much as possible. Later, when she was on her own, yet again, she would contemplate whether she had been slightly blinded by jealousy over the last couple of days.

"Para, can I say a few things before you go? Thanks for that info although I don't know what it means to me yet. I can't tell you who I work for and I don't know if trouble will come to the winery but, if it does, I promise I will let you know and you can get lover boy away from there. About the money, I promised you two hundred a day, not just to work for me but because I was dragging you away from your island and your livelihood, so here is your full pay, up to the end of the holiday. Whether you and Petros have a good time with the money or whether you save it will be up to you. Lastly, you little bitch, I can well imagine that your boobs do look ten times better in my bras than mine do, so borrow whatever you want, give them a wash and stick them back in my drawer when you're finished with them. I will send you some brand new ones, same size, in the post when I get back to Britain."

Chapter 12

The focus looked fine until she looked on the larger television screen where she could see that the column of the tripod had to be adjusted in minute movements towards the car key, the cable from the camera to the hotels thankfully modern t.v. allowing her a large scale version of her efforts. It always felt strange to be playing with a bit of kit and watching the results of your efforts on a screen, away from the kit and it made her feel a bit like a surgeon carrying out brain surgery with the area of brain being worked on, hugely magnified, on a screen. She placed the scale rule in various positions so that Pierre, or whatever his real name was, could work out each of the key's constituent peaks and troughs, the heights, the widths and the angles. It took ten individual shots to get from one end of the key to the other. The blank, that he would use to make the key from, would not be a problem as Pierre had every blank for every car, old and new. He had assured her that his key would disarm the alarm as it opened the car door.

Feeling very alone for, what felt like, the hundredth time over the last few weeks Rebecca tried to imagine where exactly she would be right now if Para had told Petros the truth, that she was free and single, that she was lonely and in need of an explosive holiday romance. Probably she would be in the middle of a four way conversation, mainly in Greek but with bits of English thrown in to include her when the Greek got difficult or too fast. She would be having a lovely meal with lovely wine then saying good night to Para and Petros while being whisked away to a strange Greek house to be made love to by a handsome Greek man until dawn. This was, of course, pure fantasy and she would never let herself get to the point where she wasn't in charge of her senses or the situation. Surely her choice of car key photography was a better choice for her though. Wasn't it? Okay, perhaps not a better choice but with a longer lasting result. Finishing the photos, she checked each one at a hundred percent size on the television screen and, happy with the results, placed them in a shareable file and sent the link to that file to Pierre. She used his e-mail address to pay him, checked again that she had a photo of the label with the parking bay number on it and another of the Saint-Emilion envelope, slipped the key into her bag and left the hotel.

Beach number two looked much different in the dark. Although it was totally abandoned it was not spooky, not frightening but peaceful and inviting. The summer night sky, that in Greece seems to shine dimly through the dark hours, with or without a moon, made all the features of the beach visible and the constant metronomic swoosh of the tiny waves added to the calmness. With her shoes in one hand she walked the length of the beach trying to walk away from the mirrored stripe of the moon on the water and failing as it followed her. Walking back again the length of the beach, she had the sea covering her ankles and splashing her calves, cooling her whole body.

There was an area of sand castles, part way up the beach, an area defined by two young brothers as their area, their city. It was an area that had not been invaded by any other person, an area not destroyed by the sea there being no tide to speak of in the Med. It was an area that the family would probably occupy again tomorrow, one that was familiar and safe to them, where Dad felt the sea was safe and he could keep an eye on both boys, an area where Mum could sunbathe and read her easy-reading English novel knowing that her man was looking after her boys to give her a break.

In a semi-religious fashion, Rebecca knelt in the sand and placed the Peugeot key into the top of one of the sand castles with the tag sticking out and mumbled "Sorry boys but one of you will get a bollocking tomorrow for taking this key from your mother's bag. I hope it doesn't spoil your holiday and most humbly apologise to you in advance."

Not feeling tired she walked the length of the beach again, feeling the sea, feeling the pull of the moon. She kicked the water hard and soaked her dress and received, in return, an unwanted flashback of doing the same as a child, probably in Barry Island, and being told off by her mother for not changing into her bathers first. She had been transported to a time before she had been abandoned, before her parents had moved to North Wales, before she had convinced them that she was old enough and mature enough to live on her own – knowing, now that she was older, that she had been too young, too immature, but what nineteen year old would admit that at such an age? Perhaps the feelings of abandonment had happened before her parents had moved, moved to follow work, moved to further their all-important careers. Perhaps that feeling of being alone was why she had agreed to hitch-hike through France with James. Perhaps she had felt rudderless, drifting through life looking for an anchor. It was funny, she mused, how, later in life, you can look back on your earlier life and interpret things that seemed to have been done spontaneously at the time. One thing she did know for certain was that when she thought that she might be able to afford it she had returned to Saint-Emilion to look for a property, had been astonished at the prices, had worked her way out of that village looking for cheaper property and had ended up some ninety miles away with a barn, a house and a vineyard that was now looked after by Marc, who took fifty per cent of her profits on making the wine. This island, this holiday, was getting her down and she needed to either establish a definite case for the winery being mixed up with drugs or go home to Cornwall and become closer to Kitto. *"Whoa, did I really just think that last thought?"*

Arriving back in the village of her hotel the shops, houses and tavernas were closed and full of noiseless shadows. Not the 'closed' of Britain, with metal shop shutters and locked doors, this village was frozen in time, the lights turned off, but everything else the same as during the day. Tables and chairs were left out with no worry of them being taken or broken by a drunken lout. Behind the taverna, she noticed as she passed that a crate of full bottles of beer had been left out either by mistake or otherwise. She smiled, knowing that if a passer-by took a bottle they would visit the taverna tomorrow morning and pay for it. She saw nobody in the village but wondered who was awake, who could not sleep in this heat, who would be gossiping in the morning, saying that the strange British woman was wandering in the dark.

At her hotel, she entered the main door that was never locked and crept along quiet corridors. She entered her room, found the camera that Para had used on her round the island trip, took out the memory card, plugged it into her laptop and downloaded all the photos into a file that she would look at tomorrow, being way too tired to do it there and then. She smiled to see that there were a hundred and thirty seven photos, Para wishing to earn her pay no doubt and, as she tried to clear her head for sleep she wondered at her luck in having her lovely X-Pro 1 camera that she had set to automatic for Para. The camera that had all the features of a professional camera, that had file sizes to rival her professional cameras and yet looked like a point and shoot tourist camera.

Hoping for a long uninterrupted sleep she drifted off and started her usual, mixed up dream sequence of grape picking when she was young, not with James but strangely with Kitto before she had met him and with Marc, her wine maker in France making wine which was full of drugs that she drank and which confused her into thinking she was the mother of two French boys with keys around their necks.

Chapter 13

Paraskevi woke suddenly out of her own dream, trying to work out what the noise was. Realising it was her phone ringing, she worked out the next step - that it was a call and not an alarm ring and then wondered where she'd left her phone the night before. She scoured her immediate area for the phone eager to find it before the ringing stopped and established, at the same time that she was in the house of Nicholias. She didn't have to worry whether her phone had woken Petros because she'd realised, at the same time, that he wasn't there. Her stomach churned and she panicked.

"Hello" she answered, in a fluster, without looking at the name on the phone.

"Can you fillet and cook fish?"

"Petros, is that you? Where the hell are you? I thought..."

Petros was talking calmly and like someone who had been awake for hours and was enjoying himself; just about the complete opposite of the feelings running through Para. A dull, rumbling, background noise sounded somewhere in the distance behind him.

"Calm yourself my goddess, I am on the little boat belonging to Alessandro, he won't mind and I will pay him for his petrol. I have eight bream from a small bay that I know of but would not tell even you of its location, it is so secret. Two will be ample for our breakfast, I will sell six on the way in, either when I beach the boat if there is anyone there waiting, or at a taverna that I know that sells fish. Get some olive oil in the pan, my lovely, dress yourself like you are when you are in my dreams and we will eat on the little table in the back courtyard of the house of Nicholias."

Para giggled into her phone, whispered for him to hurry back and hung up and only then realised that the background noise that she could hear was the boat's engine. For a minute she sat in bed still wondering if she should enjoy the flattery and praise lavished on her or whether she had just been ordered to be Petro's dream woman, one who looked nice and cooked for him. Did it matter? Petros was hooked and she was turning the handle of the fishing reel.

Rebecca's phone rang and for a while it rang in her confused dream, real life seemed like it should be hours away as if she'd only just fallen asleep, which wasn't that far from the truth. The ring seemed to get louder, jumped from the dream into reality and stopped only when she tried to grab the phone to answer it but pressed the wrong button.

It was another few minutes before she had rubbed her eyes, drunk some water and found her list of recent missed calls. Pressing on Kitto's name at the top of the list, she could hear a background noise of an engine as he answered. For some reason she ran her fingers through her hair as if it would improve Kitto's view of her, a view that he obviously didn't have.

"Kitto, you working?"

"I am indeed, times are fair-ish, we can't all be laying on a beach working on our tan, can we"

Rebecca decided to leave the illusion of her bikini clad, suntanned and oiled body in Kitto's head rather than let him know that she looked almost as wrecked as the last time he had seen her in her glorious morning state.

"Everything all right Kitto, nothing wrong back home?" She was shouting over the noise of his boat engine.

"Mackerels small, three for the price of a biggun, but can't say that's a disaster, just normal these days. No, just rang for a chat, wondered how you ended up in Greece, when you were coming back, looking forward to those drinks I was"

Rebecca remembered the text and throw away line about having a drink when she got back. She hadn't meant it to sound like a date. Had Kitto hung on to the phrase in hope?

"Met a friend in London, going on holiday alone, looked into it with a travel agent and managed to get the same flight and hotel...as her."

She didn't give a damn about the lie as the truth would have been impossible to explain to Kitto but she had concentrated on the fact that she'd added, unnecessarily, the words "as her" to the end of her reply, with a small gap before the words came out and may have even over-emphasised the fact that she hadn't travelled with a man.

"I'm sure you're having good times, don't get too drunk mind. See you when you get back."

And he was gone, possibly losing signal at his end, possibly smiling at the news just gathered. She flopped back into bed. She was not getting too drunk, not drinking much at all. Not having good times and, yes, she was looking forward to getting back to St. Ives. But was she missing St. Ives or missing Kitto. He was on her mind, yet again as she drifted back into sleep.

Para was in the kitchen area, preparing a pan, pleased with the table she had already prepared with a fresh table cloth, plates and cutlery. A morning scent emanated from a small pink rose and a large red hibiscus flower, both of which she had cut from the overgrown shrubs brightening the courtyard and she worried that they should be in a slender vase but the pint beer mug filled with water would have to do. In a tall cupboard she had found an old, once white, working piny, possibly a carpenter's piny, the type that had a loop of cloth that went around the neck and had a large pocket in the front for tools. She wrapped it around herself, almost twice, pulled in the cloth straps around her waist to give her some shape, tied it up with a bow at the front and wondered how long she could stand the roughness of the cloth against her naked body.

When Petros, her hunter-gatherer caveman, burst through the door holding up the two fish by their gills, Para kissed her man in thanks, took the fish and placed them on the wooden block. Bream she had cooked many times in the taverna for rich tourists wanting a special evening meal so this made her special breakfast even more special. This would be her most extravagant breakfast ever the cost of bream on a taverna menu staying in her head as she had them cleaned, filleted and in the pan of olive oil.

Adding a few herbs from the various pots around the garden, she moved into the courtyard corner and cut a lemon from the old tree and, ever conscious that Petros was just sitting and smiling and watching her every move. She sliced the lemon, put half in each hand, drenched the fish on each plate showing equal strength in each hand, and served after removing a few pips from the plates.

Petros was in heaven. Having been at sea his head was cleared of the night's stuffiness and his nose was being bombarded with a heady mix of rose, hibiscus, oregano, olive oil, and fish – a witch's brew if ever there was one. He was eager to start his meal but waited for the witch that had captivated him with this brew, still stood at the sink. He couldn't work out the logic of this but somehow she was looking incredibly sexy in a carpenter's apron. Washing her hands she returned to the table and they ate in silence, facing each other, staring into each other's eyes and seeing their reflections mirrored in the eyes opposite them. When the meal was finished, they stayed staring at each other, each ones breath on the other's face. Para spoke first in a soft voice, grumbling at him but smiling to show him she wasn't serious.

"You abandoned me this morning; you do not love me any more."

"Even though I am the night owl, I forced myself to rise early to find my woman food because I love her so much."

"I have finished my oily fish it was caught beautifully, thank you. Do you have work today?"

"Not until lunch time and the fish would have been nothing if it hadn't been cooked so expertly and with such love."

Petros paused and Para stood to clear the table, leaning over as she rose up, as she had done so many times. She leant enticingly towards her man, gesturing for him to return to this, her little, very private, taverna. Petros eyes flashed at the amount of bare breast he was seeing over the top of the apron and, still staring, grabbed Para's hand, lowering it and the plates, slowly back to the table. Without lifting his eyes to her face he stammered "Para, what exactly are you wearing underneath that piny?

"Absolutely nothing my love. I should take it off now that breakfast is over but I'm having trouble with the knot. Could you just help me undo the ties, or shall we wash up first?"

And the rest of their morning was spent in bed unaware and uncaring that flys were landing on the plates on the table.

Rebecca eventually woke naturally, showered and got dressed, served herself yet again with yoghourt and honey, sat on her own through breakfast in the deserted dining room of the hotel and returned to her room where she started looking at the photos that Para had taken at the winery. This time it was the laptop that had a cable to the TV and she flicked through the photos, one by one, looking for anything unusual.

Para was right, the stainless steel vats were huge and the scrap value high but she could see no computer equipment, everything seemed to be operated manually. Then she came across some strange shots taken from a higher level. Going back a few shots she worked out that there were spiral steps going around one of the vats, a bit like a helter-skelter. Returning now to the shots from high level she could see that Para had been allowed to climb to the top of these steps. There was one shot of her fellow visitors and what looked like the tour guide, all looking up and waving to the camera, one shot of the sales desk in front of the office with the woman who sold the wine waving and one of the office area. Perhaps not strangely for a winery, the office was built from partitions only with no ceiling. This would have made the office cooler, and it could share the main winery lighting, and nobody could see in as all the glazed screens had venetian blinds on them. Nobody, that was, unless they were where Para had managed to get. Intentionally or not, she had found a brilliant position to photograph from and it actually allowed Para's birds-eye shot into the area of desks and filing cabinets.

This is where Para had seen the old computer that was ancient by today's standards and, as Bec zoomed in on it she could see that it even had a slot for a floppy disk, it was that old. Keeping at the same zoom level she moved to the top left corner of the photo and started working, systematically, through the office area. After about two thirds of the area had been covered she came across what looked suspiciously like folded down wine boxes. She tried to zoom in further but failed to be able to read the words printed on the card. Zooming back out again she noticed an area of high over-exposure nearby, in a strange shape. She closed the file, opened her photo editing software and re-opened the photo to turn down the highlights.

Para and Petros were saying a fond farewell to each other before leaving, Petros for work in the harbour, Para going in the opposite direction to see her friend at the hotel and change to go out with Petros that night. It was difficult for both of them to let go of each other knowing that there would be a whole, agonising, five hours before they would be with each other again. It was Petros that finally broke away saying that he'd be late and maybe lose the work if he didn't go straight away. As he left, Para stood and watched him go, pretending that her husband was off to work and she would make her house nice for his return. Snapping back into reality she decided not to shower and to keep Petros' smell on her for as long as possible. She closed the house door from the outside and set off to see Rebecca. The walk was hot and on a dusty road but gave her lots of time to think through various scenarios of her future.

Whatever happened over the coming days Para would eventually have to go home, tell her mother everything, well nearly everything, that had happened on her holiday and let Mama decide what and how much to tell Baba. Once Mama and Baba had reached a decision and told her, then Para would either go along with it, or completely ignore them and strike out on her own, to who knew where. There were a number of possible ways this could go.

My dream, my best case scenario is that Petros comes to my island, my parents like him as he is hard working, we get engaged and both work in the taverna, we get married and the taverna supports us, our children and both sets of parents. That is a lot to ask.

A bus passed and stopped to offer Para a lift but she needed time on her own and politely refused. The bus driver tooted one of his six musical horns as he left.

Second choice perhaps would be Baba exploding and insisting that I marry Yiorgo, me leaving my island to live with Petros. Again we get married and I work in someone else's taverna, he carries on doing odd jobs and we have a happy but pretty poor life together.

An old man with a large, white moustache and a toothless grin passed her, travelling in the opposite direction accompanied by a donkey stacked too high with brush wood that he'd collected for a fire or for his oven. Luckily for the donkey it was a very light load and he probably hardly noticed the weight. The donkey man looked like he could have been looking for tourists to take pictures of him and he greeted Para warmly as they passed each other. Para was amazed that she had not realised he was there until the last moment, so deep in thought was she.

There are many more scenarios so what is at the bottom of the list. Petros says goodbye as if it has been a holiday romance and I go back to my job in my parent's taverna. In a short time I find I am pregnant after today and Baba insists I marry Yiorgo straight away, the deal being that if he wants the taverna then he takes me with someone else's child. I couldn't stand the thought of living with a man, probably despising my child so, I would come back to this island, find Petros and he denies all knowledge so I go back to a miserable existence with a husband that does not love me and I devote my life to my child.

Although she was walking in the high heat of the hours after midday, a shiver ran down Paraskevi's spine and she shook her head to come out of her trance like nightmare. Although she had always thought of Rebecca as a friend, this was all too personal to share. She was in a heady mixture of euphoria given to her by her man and fear given to her by her man also.

Para walked into the room as Rebecca was looking at the photo of the strange object, obviously unable to work out what it was.

"Kysti" Para said in Greek, naturally choosing Greek as she has been speaking her native language all day.

Although a technical word, not used in tourist Greek, Rebecca had heard the word before, strangely, and related it to somebody she knew with a urinary tract infection.

"You want a wee?" She said to a puzzled Para.

"Ochi, no, I do not know it in English, it is too difficult, but we have them in our taverna."

Rebecca looked up her on-line dictionary and found the word.

"Bladder," said Rebecca to Para who was staring into the air, still deep in thought, on another planet.

"Yes, that sounds right. It is a skin full of wine to go into the wine boxes that they don't produce here apparently. See where this side of the bladder is raised in the picture? It is because the bladder is upside down, the plastic tap is underneath there but you can't see it. This bit..." Para was pointing to a protruding bit from the bladder, made from the same shiny material. "Is where they put the wine in and then they seal it. But I have never seen two filling bits before."

Rebecca was impressed. "You seem to be an expert on wine bladders Para, I would have thought that all you saw in your taverna was the outside of the boxes."

"Well, I can explain to you but it depends if I am helping my friend or talking to the police."

"Para, come on, not that again, please help me, you know I am after bigger fry than bladder tampering in a taverna!"

"Okay, the winery would buy the bladders with that protrusion open, fill the bladder with wine and heat seal it closed. On the internet you can get a tool to open the seal, put in more wine without air to spoil it and seal it again but with a thing like you get in the back of your hand in hospital to be opened to give you drugs, but no air, and then it's closed up again."

Rebecca was nodding "A venflon" she said and then added "So you can add cheaper wine to the box?"

Paraskevi was horrified and insulted. "No, that would be bad. What we do is all good for everyone. I will explain. Box wine is usually cheaper wine and we keep it behind the counter for lonely people like you Rebecca who only want one glass of wine, or maybe a small carafe that can be filled from the box. Many couples who are not lonely have a bottle of good wine, get greedy and order a second but only drink half the bottle, leaving half a bottle on the table. When we add that half bottle to the wine box we improve the quality of the wine for the next person. So, like so many things in Greece, nobody loses, everyone gains and all is well with the world."

Rebecca was impressed, tried to remember what the boxed wine tasted like in Para's taverna and tried to remember to later complain to her about being called lonely even though it was true.

"But why would you have two entry points? It doesn't make sense."

Para tutted as if she was talking to a child or someone who was too dull to see the obvious.

"I haven't a clue Bec, unless perhaps there are two entry points into two compartments in the bladder and someone wanted to fill a top compartment with drugs and a separate bottom compartment with wine so that if anyone was suspicious of a drug filled wine box and turned on the tap then wine would come out. Of course nobody would be suspicious anyway, especially sniffer dogs as, if it was me, I would put the full bladder through the bottle sterilising line that they conveniently have in the winery to rid the outside of any trace of the drug. I don't know but I wonder if the bladder happened to be x-rayed, if it would show up as a solid metal object because it is made of shiny aluminium? Oh, and don't forget your promise. I do not want Petros anywhere near any of this. These boys are guards, paid a pittance. Nothing to do with smuggling drugs"

Rebecca was utterly astounded. It is one of those things, she told herself, that was obvious once you knew.

"My promise is good. I have to follow the smugglers through Italy to France and, once they are caught with the people they are delivering to then I will ring you before I tell anyone within the police. I promise. The only thing is I don't know when they are leaving and only know part of their route so may easily lose them."

Rebecca revealed some of the details about the family she'd been watching and told her that their surname was Jeune and showed Para the photos of the number plate and the envelope address in St. Emilion.

Para tutted for a second time which hinted to Bec that Para was really earning Bec's salary and would need favours in return. Picking up her phone she entered the number for the car hire company, advertised in the photo of the number plate, dialled and started talking in very fast Greek.

"Hi, hotel reception here, I have my client Kyrie Jeune here, he is unaware of where to return the hire car with the following registration."

She read out the registration's Greek letters and numbers and awaited a reply, writing it down for Bec as she listened.

"Hi, tell Kyrie Jeune please that when he brings the car to the port on Tuesday 4th July, there will be our rep to meet him. He must however leave time for our rep to inspect the car before the family boards the 2.00pm catamaran. Our rep will be there at one."

After the usual pleasantries the call was ended and Para explained her notes to Bec and the fact that she had a week before the French family left. It could have been an awkward silent afternoon with Para not wanting to discuss her feelings for Petros and her worry for her life to come and with Bec sat trying to work out how to get ahead of the family, how to follow someone through a country and what to do at the drugs exchange. Instead, that one word from Para, the Greek for bladder, had sorted Bec out completely and she decided to discuss more with Para even though she could see that Para's head was elsewhere, presumably on planet love. She shared what she thought would be alright for Para to know and promised herself that later she would be less selfish and would ask Para whether she was deeply in love, or whether they had just split up. One of these scenarios would explain Para's head floating in space.

"Bec, I don't mean to tell you what to do but, instead of hiring a car to drive through Italy trying not to lose them, why don't you fly Athens to Paris, hire a car there, drive to their home and sit outside their house and wait for them to get home? You have their address I think you said?"

"That's a fantastic idea and I was thinking along those lines myself." She lied. "Of course, as soon as I leave, Petros can move in here and Nicholias can have his house back."

They smiled, knowingly at each other and Bec had established, without asking, that Para was still madly in love and still with her man. Bec was tired through lack of sleep after being woken by Kitto, Para was tired after a morning of sex and walking so a siesta was agreed and well deserved and Bec left Para's head to return slowly to Earth on its own.

Chapter 14

It was a time for taking stock of the situation
that Bec found herself in. She was sat up in bed
with only her laptop for company. Para had been
whisked away the night before by Petros as soon as
he had finished work, negating the need for Bec to
listen to too much detail about their relationship.
By the way they giggled away together it was
obvious to Bec that Para's head was floating in
deep love and that she should be grateful that Para
had been focussed enough to help her solve her
case. She had a sheet of used paper and a pen by
her side and had already drawn columns on the
clear side of the sheet, each column being a day.
She would work out what would happen each day
for the French family and their travels home, then
each day for her travels and then, once worked
out, it would all go into her diary.

Her diary on her laptop was linked to the
diaries on her tablet and on her smart phone so
she was never without it. Someone had said once
that it was annoying if someone rang you on your
mobile to ask if you were free on a certain day and
you would have to end the call, look at your diary
on your phone and then ring them back. Bec
could remember thinking that it never happened
to her because she didn't get such phone calls.

Today was Tuesday 27th June. With the French family leaving in a weeks time Rebecca calculated, or her laptop calculated, that they would arrive in St. Emilion late on the evening of the following Saturday 8th July. If she left Para and this island today she could stop off at her villa, spend the night, get back to her holiday hotel by the following evening, have a luxurious bath and comfortable bed and enjoy two days of relaxation and sunbathing before flying back to Bristol to arrive very early on this Saturday morning coming.

That schedule would give her a week to re-establish herself in St.Ives, fly to France, make camp at 'The Chateau' as she called it, her cottage with pretensions of being a chateau attached to her vineyard, and then she could drive to St. Emilion to meet the French family at their house. She would arrive at the Jeune's house on the Saturday morning and wait the day for them, just in case they had made good time. Happy with the plan, happy with the entries into her diary, she concentrated on the finer detail. Annoyingly she planned to arrive in St. Emilion first thing on the Saturday morning to wait for her target's arrival knowing that she would probably not be able to park in the narrow streets and that she would be stood on a street corner, waiting, for the best part of a day. She was conscious that she was taking her eye off the task in hand by planning ahead with fine detail. Sending an e mail to her favourite St.

Ives restaurant, she booked a table for two on the Saturday of her arrival in St. Ives. She requested a table number that she knew was in a cosy corner, she knew the restaurant that well.

Rising, showering and dressing, she achieved breakfast at breakfast time for the first time since arriving to find that there were actually other guests staying and then she went to find the hotel owner (there was no desk) and asked that if she left and let Paraskevi stay for the duration paid for, could Para's male friend take Bec's place in the room and at breakfast. She received a shoulder shrug and a smile from the lady hotel owner, a shrug that meant "what do I care as long as I have my money. Am I your friends mother that I should worry she is with this boy?" So she returned to her room and rang Para to explain her plans – up to the point where she got back to St. Ives and missing out France completely.

An e mail came in. "Table booked. Anyone I know?"

Bec smiled, cheeky she thought and e mailed back "Yes. That should keep you wondering for a while."

There was just one more thing for Bec to do and then she would be able to start packing to leave for her holiday hotel. Back into e mail she found, listed under Jenny, the e mail address of the local hairdresser that she visited on too few occasions and should really visit more often. "Jenny, on holiday in Greece, hair full of salt and chlorine, nails snapped and ragged, skin as hairy as a lumberjack. Need rescuing a week Saturday. Can be with you by about 10 but it could take you all day to make me look human again. By the way, need hair up, fancy but not a wedding."

Someone, perhaps Jenny, was sat on the computer in the salon. They were probably going through a slack period, the reply was almost immediate. "Booked in from 10 until 3, you make it sound horrendous. Pedicure also? Bikini line or more? Is this for anyone I know?"

For the second time today she read "Anyone I know" and her mind jumped back to the day she left St. Ives and the thought of everyone knowing everyone's business. It is a friendly place, an over friendly place but Para had taught her that she needed to be in her friendly place. Bec was beginning to admit that she was too alone, too isolated.

Thanks to high speed catamarans Rebecca had said goodbye to Paraskevi, and was on her way. After changing boats at a beautiful island that she promised herself she would revisit one day, she had landed at the island of her Greek home. There she had packed away her walking stick microphone and video camera equipment and sat

204

counting the stash of Euros in her safe into many piles, each pile of a thousand. She needed this figure to enter into a calculation at a later date. As there was no rush she decided to spend the night there, and sat on her bed, her head whirring with travel and thoughts of wineries, drugs and Para's happiness.

Rebecca hated procrastination and forced herself to pick up her mobile, shaking like a schoolgirl, scared of being rejected, of being laughed at, at being hurt.

"Kitto, can you hear me, about that drink Saturday, do you fancy a meal instead? Catch up on gossip?"

There. She'd done it. She'd asked Kitto out on a date. A faint voice came back and Bec held her breath, still shaking.

"That you Bec, hang on, can't hear a bloody thing, live band. You stay where you are, I'll go outside."

Kitto had been drinking and Bec got nervous. Perhaps this was a stupid idea, he would probably be working Saturday night anyway, depending on the tides.

"That's better, can hear myself think now. Bec, you still there I'm by the wooden door next to pub, one with paint peeling off, tourists take pictures of it, you know the one. You ok? You still on holiday?

Bec had a picture in her head of a door with green peeling paint, shot in strong cross light with deep shadows, a photo in an old magazine she had kept. The tourist photos of the door Kitto was stood at were all taken in flat light and would be discarded when the tourists got back home from their holidays. Remembering the reason for her call she snapped back into reality, her nervousness gone and spurted out;

"Holidays great but getting a bit boring. About the drink Saturday, if you're still on, I'm getting fed up of Greek food and fancy something like a steak. Do you fancy a meal after the drink; I can book it from this end. Of course if you're working...?"

The beer had given Kitto confidence enough to come back with a Smart Alec reply.

"Let me weigh up my options here. Joey mackerel – meal with a beautiful woman – joey mackerel – meal with a beautiful woman. Okay Bec, you just about win, The Ketch at seven was it?"

Rebecca laughed at Kitto but realised that she had chickened out and said the reason she wanted a steak with him was merely because she was fed up of Greek food. In the relief of not making a fool of herself and decided to push her luck.

"What if it hadn't been joey mackerel? What if full grown mackerel were being caught?"

"Have to think about that one, tell you over a steak."

She finished the call, used her pool to cool down and think before drifting off to sleep, thankful that her days of walking to beaches were over, thankful that she had a friend. Thankful for the dreams she had that night, dreams of a nature that she hadn't had for a while.

Chapter 15

The next morning Rebecca woke early, plugged in her laptop and started tidying files. There were written files containing addresses and parts of transcriptions of videos, the actual video files of the French family and photo files of the winery. She looked at each one, tidied them up, merged them into one file and moved the large file to her updatable file sharing system. This would give her access to all these files from her laptop, her tablet and her phone in case they were needed over the next week or so. If she updated anything on one piece of kit it would update on the other two bits of kit and, more importantly than anything else, when she sent the lot to Geordie, it would undergo encryption at her end and his end so that only he would ever see the files that she sent. By the time it left her it would incriminate the winery, the French family and, hopefully, the people in Paris where the drugs ended up. The tidying up of the files took the best part of the morning and, when it was time for lunch, she realised that lunch could not be eaten here as there was no food and no Paraskevi to stock the fridge. As she exited the door and left for the harbour to find a taverna and lunch, she looked back at the unmade bed and wondered whether Para would ever return to clean the room and work in her parent's taverna or if she would start a new life with Petros on his island.

Lunch on the harbour side was as relaxed and cool as any Greek lunch should be and because of the catamaran times it was extended into mid-afternoon. The speed of the catamaran removed all feeling of floating slowly through life and it dumped her at the island of the hotel paid for by Geordie where, it seemed, hundreds of taxi drivers shouted at her that theirs was the best car to take her to the big hotel where, if you could afford to stay there then you could afford a big tip. Rebecca compared travelling from a small Greek island to the shock of this tourist centre with the difference between St. Ives and London.

After a protracted conversation with a hotel receptionist, who believed that she wanted to check in and couldn't understand that she was already staying and that she'd gone absent but with leave to go, she managed to get her key from a receptionist with better English. Life was further complicated by the fact that Bec really only had one and a half days left in the hotel, had to be out of her room by midday, wanted to pay for the last afternoon and to keep her room on before leaving for home – which would be in the evening, on the tourist company coach. Eventually it was all organised, she was handed her key-card, she showered, was in silk shorts and top pyjamas from the draw of her room where everything had stayed untouched and she was dropping off to sleep in a double bed that was all hers and where she was able to stretch and turn at will. It was time to relax for two whole days starting tomorrow, to forget about the winery, forget about the French family, forget about Para's love life and just relax.

On the way to the pool, the following morning, Bec sat in her beach wrap in the library alcove of the hotel reception and looked for a book that would take her away from reality. She looked through all the usual suspects, the novels that she would normally choose that were the ones branded "Shortlisted for the such and such prize" but was not tempted. All these books, bought in various airports and now discarded were beautifully written but would not allow her the instant escape she craved. Knowingly judging a book by its cover, she picked up a book that looked as if she wouldn't have to concentrate too much on it, the cover showing a couple in romantic embrace, and she wandered to the same sun beds and umbrella that she had claimed over a week ago, settling down to a day of relaxation and a world where the men had deeply penetrating eyes that made women hearts flutter, their breath to intake and their stomachs to have empty bits in them. The novel, as she had hoped, was so relaxing that she drifted off to sleep only to be woken by a burning feeling on her right foot that was not covered by the umbrella now that the sun had reached its midday height. Lunch was cool and air conditioned and she even allowed herself a beer or two before reclaiming her sun bed once the sun had lost some of its ferocity.

She stood in her bikini to lower the umbrella. She fumbled a bit with the umbrella's workings, got caught in the innards of the umbrella and covered by the canvas so decided that she was probably the opposite of the stick insect women that she had watched posing at the start of her holiday. Returning to her book she realised that she hadn't got very far into it but wouldn't be too bothered to be leaving it, tomorrow night, back in the library only half read.

Bec looked up from her page, looked over the top of her sunglasses and moved her head to the left, to the position where the man had invaded her space and sat on the bed next to her, staring at her and waiting to speak.

"I apologise lady, I see you beautiful from my bed other side pool, I wonder why beautiful lady alone, if she want company if I can share a drink with her."

His eyes were penetratingly blue, unusual for the Greek that he undoubtedly was and the deep sexy voice coming out of the very handsome face was well practiced and the huge gold chain around his neck was real. Bec waited for her heart to flutter. It didn't. She checked that she was awake and not in her novel. She was awake. She has had no intake of breath; there were no pits in her stomach. Checks completed she lifted her mobile from her side.

"Would you mind if I rang my husband to ask him, he doesn't always like that sort of thing?"

Blue eyes grinned without blushing, rose without speaking, tilted his head to the side to indicate 'ah well, I tried but failed' and returned to his sun bed and Rebecca returned to her book, although she was staring at the page without reading.

She was thinking about his blue eyes, not because they were nice but because Greeks saw blue eyes as unlucky, perhaps because it showed a past where there had been a mixing of races outside Greek culture. Even today, baby's blankets or clothing had a blue eye pinned to them and adults wore them on necklaces and bracelets. It depended on which culture you were from but on some islands it was pinned on a baby to stop it forming blue eyes, on some it was to ward off evil spirits and, on the more modern islands, it was just for good luck. Rebecca thought that when she returned to her room she would dig out her blue eye ring, not for good luck but to ward off the evil spirit that she saw in this man. She believed him to be more than a chancer.

She could see the waiter taking orders around the pool and it was nearly her turn as numbers had thinned out and there wasn't anyone on the beds around her. She reached for her bag, took out her purse and found a fifty Euro note. She held it in her hand close to her side but where the waiter could see it. He was just about to tell her that all drinks were within the all inclusive cost but Rebecca spoke first.

"I know it's a bit late but I would like a cappuccino and some information please."

The waiter looked down at the fifty, realised that this was serious information required and said, in impeccable English "I will try my best on both counts madame."

Rebecca continued "A man just tried to chat me up, I will describe him shortly, I would like to know his name and where he is from please."

The waiter smiled "I'm sure that's possible madam, you don't have to describe him if he is wearing a heavy gold chain around his neck, he recently asked me if you were alone and if you were the lady that arrived by taxi last night. I told him yes because he offered me a tip that didn't

213

materialise so perhaps you might like to know that he also arrived by taxi, shortly after you."

With that the waiter turned and walked away to retrieve the required information and the cappuccino and Rebecca stared through sun glasses at 'blue eyes' over the top of her book.

When the waiter returned he offered her a silvered tray bearing a cappuccino in a tall glass on a coaster and a coaster next to it, under his thumb to stop it blowing away. He released his thumb and Rebecca read Angelos Savas from Pothanaramos followed by a mobile number.

"A small island a day away from here." Explained the waiter. "The mobile number is mine though, I don't get that many tips, certainly not 50s and you may require further information."

Rebecca glanced at the waiters name badge. "Stay on my side Henry, I will probably need more help from you and have some more 50s in my purse. I will call your mobile now and immediately hang up so you will have my number and can help me leave tomorrow without that horrible man seeing me go."

Rebecca knew the island that Mr. Savas was from, Rebecca had just left there, had left Para there, now her heart fluttered, her stomach churned but for all the wrong reasons. She would spend the night in broken sleep worrying. Had blue eyes been in her room searching? Did he want to know how much she knew about the winery? Had he come to scare her off or even kill her? How could she get home alive? How had anyone from the winery found out that Rebecca knew anything and where was Para in all this?

Chapter 16

Paraskevi and Petros spent one night in the hotel that had been paid for by Rebecca and were contemplating ringing Nicholias and offering him money if they could go back to his double bed. They had tried sleeping in one of the single beds; they had pushed the two singles together to make a double. Nothing was working. Perhaps their love life was too young and active for two singles; perhaps Petros was falling down through the gap between the two beds to prove a point. They lay in their respective beds, facing each other, frustrated.

"There is, of course, an alternative, but it would involve a huge commitment from you Petros and I do not think you are ready for that but I will say it anyway." Para was talking as if she had just thought of something and hadn't been working towards this point for the last couple of days.

"In my dreams we both go back to my island. My mother would accept you straight away as she would see from my actions that I was in love with you. My father, of course, would not accept you, would see you as a money grabber after his taverna, a chancer after his daughter, a trouble maker causing trouble between his family and the family of Yiorgo to who I am promised."

"You make your father sound really nice to meet; you are tempting me with his friendliness," was Petros' sarcastic reply.

"Oh, there's more to scare you. You would have to work alongside me in the taverna, with me as your boss, telling you what to do, with my father criticising your every move and, and here comes the big one, you, with the help of my mother, would have to get my father's permission for you to marry me so that we could be engaged and live together in the same bedroom. This point is where I could maybe start crying as I have scared you and you walk out of my life."

Petros held Para tightly trying hard not to slip through the gap between the beds.

"There is no need for you to cry my beauty. I am not leaving your life. I am ready to take on your father so that we can spend our lives together but there is one huge obstacle in front of us that I think you have not thought through and that could spoil everything."

Paraskevi sat up, her head searching for what she had missed, searching but not finding so eventually she asked Petros what it was.

"You remember how you attacked me when I translated your Paraskevi name as Friday and said you were my Girl Friday. My surname that I give to you on our wedding day is Avgerinos. Your name Paraskevi Avgerinos sounds like the name of a weekend newspaper. The Friday Morning Star – do you want to sound like the title of a weekend newspaper."

Paraskevi laughed uncontrollably through relief. She had not thought about a change of name but was thrilled to find that Petros had given it thought.

"Not good, I will have to marry one of your friends instead, one with a better name."

"Or, I could take the name of my mother when I am on your island. Dallaras. How does that grab you? Paraskevi Dallaras. Plus I think we are close enough now for you to call me Pedro as all my friends do as Petros is too formal."

And so Petros Avgerinos was thereafter known to Para as Pedro Dallaras and she felt powerful in that by arguing over a name she had confirmed her marriage to the father of any baby that resulted from their unprotected holiday love making.

Rebecca on the other hand was not laughing, was not thinking of marriage or unprotected sex. She was concentrating on getting out of her hotel alive.

"Henry, is that you, I'm sorry to ring at such an hour, are you still on duty?"

"No, I am at home with my family until tomorrow morning but I told my wife about the lady that tips so well so she won't mind that you ring me."

"Sorry. I need a huge favour that has a tip attached to it. On your way into work tomorrow morning can you get me a home hair dye kit for blonde hair please and get it to my room. Also, if you are still on duty tomorrow night, can you try and find a group of women going into town and explain to them that I want to leave the bar with them to share a taxi into town. I will pay for the taxi and leave them on getting to their chosen club. Do all of this and there's a 100 bill for you."

"Consider it done." Was Henry's reply and that meant that Rebecca could at least sleep a little easier even though she had locked her balcony doors, placed a chair in front of them and put the chain on her room door for the first time.

In the morning she packed. Her case was ready to go and her travel bag with passport and tickets was inside the case. All that she had left – unpacked - were the bikini and sarong that she stood up in, heels, a glam short length dress with plunging neckline to leave the hotel in, going out underwear, an old tee shirt that she could bin before leaving and a large handbag that contained her purse, a rolled up top, rolled up baggy trousers and flat shoes.

Henry knocked, saw her in her bikini and refused to come in in case he was compromised.

"I will stay by here by the door; my wife already has suspicions about the size of your tips and what I am doing to gain them. I hope this hair colour is what you wanted; it's the first time I've bought anything like this. I've spoken to three bubbly women who go into town every night. I told them you were meeting someone in town and were scared to take a taxi on your own. They were sympathetic, and then I told them you were paying for the taxi, and then they were enthusiastic. They leave the hotel bar at eight."

"Thank you Henry, here's your 100. Can you please order a taxi for 7.45, arrange for my cases to be taken down at 7.45 and put in the taxi boot. Explain to the driver to charge me from when my cases go in, we will go to town then the airport."

"Of course, now perhaps you can understand why I could not come in. When a lady pulls a 100 bill from her bikini bottom it makes me a bit hot and nervous."

Bec laughed, pushed him away, told him he was a good friend and sat to read the hair dye instructions that were, not very helpfully, in Greek.

Surprisingly there was only one word that she had to use a dictionary for. It was the word for an allergy test and angered Bec as she had no intention of carrying one out and was more concerned with survival of life. She followed the instructions one by one, dressed in the old tee shirt and when the hair colour was complete and the hairstyle roughed, the clothes were added. Glasses were chosen, being wire rimmed sunglasses with the lenses taken out and Bec looked into a full length mirror. Was she looking at someone a good ten, or twelve years younger than she actually was, or was it an obvious case of mutton dressed as lamb in a dress that was too short? In either case the disguise worked and her plan was rolling itself out. She reminded herself of the couple in Bristol Airport that could not be suspicious as they didn't blend in and stood out in their finery. The idea was that she would leave the hotel, glammed up, drink in hand, giggling and the centre of attention. Nothing for blue eyes to worry about there then.

Just before the appointed time she ordered, from room service, a giant, flamboyant cocktail complete with an umbrella and straw. Taking a deep drink through the straw, partly for confidence, partly to show she was not just starting the drink, she descended in the lift, following the route her cases had earlier taken. She easily found the three bubbly women warming up for their trip into town and decided that they were roughly the age of the woman Bec had earlier seen in the mirror. The four of them laughed, they joked and eventually they walked through the large hotel reception. They were stared at by blue eyes and his enquiring, searching, gaze but he didn't see what he was looking for he just saw long bare legs on stupid tourist women. A minute later the women were in the taxi.

With the giggly Northern English women dropped off in town Bec moved from the front seat into the rear and asked the driver to head for the airport with all haste. In her excellent tourist Greek she asked the driver to tilt his mirror as she needed to get changed. He replied in equally good Greek that he didn't understand, grinned with an evil expression and waited in anticipation for the strip show. He was disappointed as Bec decided to change in the airport toilet. For some reason unknown to the taxi driver she didn't want to incite being attacked in the back of a taxi by a driver driven mad by the sight of a Brit in her sexy underwear.

Changed in a cubicle that could only just accept her and her case she headed to baggage drop and queued behind three boys whose white skinindicated that they had not seen any sun during their holiday. Listening to their over loud banter she established that they were totally broke, were from South Wales and were arguing over which one would use their credit card for the car park, the needed petrol and for the Severn Bridge Toll. As she smiled at their dilemma she noticed blue eyes scanning the crowd and immediately offered the boys a solution that would suit everyone.

"Boys mun" she opened the conversation establishing with them in two simple words that they all had a common South Wales bond. "I've got a plan that'll benefit us all if you're interested. I'm being chased by a holiday fling who wants to marry me and says he will kill either me or himself if I leave him. He can't find me because I've dyed my hair but he's going through the queues looking for women on their own. I need one of you to put my arm through theirs, to be with me until all the bags are checked in and we get to duty free, the other two will need to stay in front of us and when we get to duty free there's a hundred quid in it for you to share."

The group leader, looking a bit older than the other two, stepped up "I feel I already know you" He said, a bit too cockily for Rebecca's liking and they chatted, arm in arm until duty free, Rebecca fending off any suggestions that there might be a continuation of the exercise. Bec took her seat on the plane; her pre-booked seat being away from the boys, and sat contemplating how much in money it had taken to get away from blue eyes and what the hell her hairdresser was going to say when she saw her the following day. Sleep on the plane came easily as she had undergone disturbed sleep the night before. On landing at Bristol and catching the train to Cornwall she soon found herself at home, her case in her flat, and sat in the hairdresser's chair, listening to gossip and being told that hairdressers absolutely love home hair dye kits as they very often have to rescue clients from them when they go wrong, so they bring in lots of extra work.

She was advised that as the new colour was so new it was probably advisable to grow it out slowly but with the addition of lowlights from time to time. Everyone in the salon agreed though that the blonde hair went well with her tanned skin and the youngest assistant suggested blue coloured contact lenses to finish the look but Rebecca kindly declined. She emerged with her hair still blonde but no longer roughed up, it was in a tasteful hair up style. With her skin waxed absolutely all over, having been forced to do the very private bits herself in a noisy masochistic ritual, and with false finger nails that looked so sharp they could kill, she was ready for action.

Chapter 17

John and Big Ray had already been in The Ketch for over an hour when Kitto arrived and, as they needlessly told him, he was in his posh clobber. They got him the half pint that he asked for but then teased him about why he was staying sober and about the shirt that actually had a collar, something not known to have been in Kitto's wardrobe and an item that he had obviously gone out and bought especially for the occasion. Big Ray offered to go home and get his dicky bow for Kitto to borrow and John swore he could smell mackerel somewhere but couldn't make out where it was coming from because of the overpowering smell of 1980's after shave. Kitto was used to their banter but it wasn't exactly calming his nerves as he sat with his drink wondering when the last time was that he'd gone out for a meal with a female of any age.

"What's all this with halves anyway. You'll be drinking cocktails next." Laughed John and then Big Ray dug Kitto in the ribs and nodded towards the door.

Rebecca stood facing them and looked stunning. She was wearing the same tight jeans, white shirt and killer heels that she had been wearing on the night that Kitto had saved her but this time her hair was blonde and was up off her face apart from a sexy little wisp that purposely hung loose over a suntanned face her makeup having been professionally applied. Kitto was oblivious to all of that, could not have worked it out for himself and just knew she looked gorgeous and recognised the tight jeans that he loved. The three lads stood up automatically and in unison and John told Kitto "Close that mouth Kitto you look like your catching flies" and Big Ray said "You look cracking Bec, we'd love to stay but tide don't wait for man so me and John need to get off. You'll be gentle with our mate now, wont you."

Kitto blushed and pushed at his friends to leave saying "Clear off you two and let two old friends catch up on gossip."

They shuffled out, giggling like schoolboys that knew that the pair they were leaving behind had each dressed for more than a gossip. Kitto asked Bec what she wanted to drink and waited for what seemed an eternity for an answer. Bec was feeling great and soaking in the moment. She had already been feeling confident in her appearance, but to be able to stun into silence three, usually jokey men, boosted that confidence even further. This was a different Bec to the one that had, apparently, stood in this pub ranting about meat, nude paintings and her saving the world from the evil of man.

"Shall we stick to wine tonight?" Bec suggested "Michael has some lovely ones at his place, we could go straight up there. The table's booked for ten minutes time" Then she looked at Kitto's drink almost completely hidden in his large hand "I can't imagine your enjoying that half pint. If we wander up there slowly you can fill me in on the local news from while I've been away."

Kitto agreed, wondered if he had enough cash in his wallet for 'nice wine' as well as food and they left straight away.

The walk was slow and uphill and they walked at arms length from each other as friends should. The gradient reminded Rebecca of the many steps to the castle taverna where the Greek dancing had taken place. She remembered the exertion of walking uphill in the heat, trying not to sweat before sitting down for a meal and thought about how similar tonight was. By the time they got to the brightly coloured, restaurant, Bec had been filled in on the ever decreasing mackerel catches, the two weddings that had happened while she'd been away, Kitto's niece's christening and Paul McGregor suddenly moving to Padstow but nobody knowing why but suspecting a local married woman was involved. Kitto panicked a bit as he wondered what the hell they were going to talk about for the rest of the night over the course of the meal.

Their table was ready for them, and they scanned the menus, nervously, decided between them not to have a starter, both independently chose the rib eye steak for main and Kitto asked Bec to choose the wine. She asked the waiter for an old vintage Rioja and explained to the waiter that they would have the wine now, while they chatted and waited for their food.

"Kitto, have you realised that if I bump into you anywhere and we chat, it's always about other people, just like tonight's chat. I know absolutely nothing about you other than the fact that you fish."

"Well I know even less about you. Seems to me you get paid loads of money to go on foreign holidays. I'd love a job like that."

Rebecca had a standard description of her job for people who asked her about it, which was a total lie but believable and shrouded in the secrecy that she needed. They were both feeling a bit nervous with each other so Rebecca decided that, as she had a rehearsed answer, it would be better for her to go first.

"Well, you know the woman on the telly, the one that finds property for couples abroad and they sometimes pick one of her choices to buy, well my job is a bit like that but without the telly. The woman on the box is usually talking 50k, 60k, my clients are talking millions in some cases. I get recommended by word of mouth, then I spend a day or two with the couple finding out about them, what they are looking for and what I think they should be looking for, and then, when we are all agreed I go and look for what the wife wants (she'll make the final decision) with a slight nod towards what the husband with the wallet wants. I am known for my discretion, never reveal who I've worked for or what they have paid me, and I get paid a percentage of the finished house cost, which is great especially if I'm involved with the interior design. I might, for instance (and this happened a year ago) come back to a client and say that I've found three large adjacent properties in a town on a hill in Tuscany. The asking price is three quarters of a million, it would take about half a million to a million to knock them into one and refurbish them to a high standard and that the finished product would be worth between two and a half and three million. Then we all go and look at it, the wife will fall in love with the potential of her new nest that she can build from scratch and show off to her friends, the husband will fall in love with the potential profit to be had and a deal will be done. I know it sounds glamorous but none of the money is mine, none of the property is mine, I am just a scout looking for other people."

"Wow" Kitto was impressed. "Almost as glamorous as my life fishing then."

Bec smiled, poured another glass of wine for them both and pushed Kitto into an answer. "Come on Kitto, I know fishing takes up a lot of time and you're governed by tide times and I know that you meet your mates in the pub a lot, but what else is there about you."

"Well, I read a lot" he sounded almost apologetic, "hell of a lot really. That means when I'm in the pub and the lads are talking football I'm a bit left out as I don't like the game much. The lads don't seem to read as much as me unless it's the sports pages."

Bec jumped in "That's fantastic, I've met a bloke who doesn't want to talk about football, go on then, types of book? Mystery? Fantasy? Favourite author?"

"Read philosophy a lot. Can't discuss that in local pub usually, can't even admit to it to a lot of people really."

"What, like Plato and Socrates and that?"

"Yeah them, Socrates, Plato and Aristotle if you want them in right order but more modern guys too and those in between."

Rebecca was fascinated, this was a totally new area for her. Looking at and listening to Kitto she would never have guessed his interests.

By now they were into their steaks and chatting between mouthfuls but Bec could not let the subject drop and Kitto was pleased to find someone who was interested in him. Bec finished a chip, ordered a second bottle of Rioja and asked "How easy would it be for you to pick a philosopher that you like, pick a book or a theory and explain it to me in words I can actually understand. I'm warning you, it will have to be very basic for me to be able to follow it."

"Nobody asked that before but I can tell you about a book changed my life or the way I look at my life, if you like, changed the way I make decisions. Clever bloke called Nietzsche wrote lots of books, one where he pretends to be old time Greek like the ones you just said. Anyway, the gist of part of the book condensed right down. Imagine, you, Rebecca, live your life and die. Soon as you die your born again into exactly the same life and know everything that's going to happen in your life, minute by minute, the good times, the bad things you've done, the boring things you've done, everything. He's not saying this happens mind, just to try and imagine if it did. You could be lying in bed thinking tomorrow is the day when I lie to my friend and then they find out the day after and I lose that friend, you'd be wishing that it had never happened. Now imagine that every time you die, your life happens over and over for ever."

Rebecca was horrified at the thought but also fascinated imagining, not Groundhog Day but Groundhog Life. Bits of her life that she would hate to see repeated, passed in front of her. It would be horrible to go into a relationship knowing how, and when, it was going to end, waiting for the inevitable to happen.

"Here's the clever bit though." He continued "What if you, at your age now, knew this continuing life was going to happen after you died. What would you change or do in your life to come so you didn't regret it next time around, or the time after that? What would you do that you wouldn't mind happening over and over again? That you would love to happen over and over again? How would your life change?"

Rebecca felt oddly freed from a shackle. Kitto's life had been changed by this book, perhaps hers would be also, without even reading the book or knowing its title. Something she had been planning, quietly, over the last week or so, no longer felt so stupid and even felt believable. The major brain shift she yearned for that might give her a happier life appeared possible.

"Shall we skip pudding and go" she asked a surprised Kitto.

Kitto wondered if he'd bored her and reached for his wallet.

"No, there's no need, I have an account. I eat here regularly on my own, Michael sends me a monthly bill and I pop up here with the cash. I am the world's worst cook." Then putting her hand on top of Kitto's hand she went for broke. Either her life would change for the better or she would ruin the one real friendship she had in this life. "Kitto, there's something I want to share with you which is not easy to say, and if I've misjudged the situation then I'm going to look really stupid but I'm quite good at that as you already know. At the moment I'm wishing I had more wine on board to make me a bit braver.

All my life, through school, with my parents, through my working life, I've been in charge. In the jobs I've had where I've been in charge of people, in my home life where I've insisted on a minimum of fifty percent of decisions, money, property, you know what I mean. One of the reasons that I took up photography was to have a fifty per cent chance against men within my agency because the photos were judged without a name attached to them. Call it controlling, call it feminism, call it wanting equality, call it what you want. Basically, over the last few weeks I've decided that I'm totally pissed off with that life, it hasn't worked for me, it hasn't made me happy, it's made me sad, friendless and very lonely and I am going for a big change in my life."

233

Rebecca took a drink of her wine. Kitto looked concerned but said nothing as he knew that she hadn't finished and wouldn't want to be interrupted so he let her continue.

"Do you remember the phrase you said to me the other day that went something like, I like my women to be at least semi-conscious, thank you very much? Well I feel a bit tiddly with the wine but much more than half conscious tonight, glowing with the red Rioja but not out of it like I was back then. I would be thrilled if you would demonstrate to me how exactly you threw me over your shoulder like a Viking with a captured wench from ancient Britain, how you carried me upstairs in my own home and then could you act out what your fantasy was as you lay on my settee and imagined that you had actually raped and pillaged me instead of looking after me. Or do you really want to stay for pudding? Michael does a really nice Eton Mess."

Paraskevi also was enjoying a meal but not the romantic two person meal that her friend was enjoying. It had started with her and Petros in the harbour-side taverna but tables kept on being added as, all through their meal, members of Petros's group came and went, usually on mopeds, sometimes stopping to eat, sometimes stopping to chat with a lot of whispered conversation going on. Para thought it was like a big family meal and couldn't, at any one point, recite the names of who was seated, the list changed so often. The surprise though came when they all arrived back at the house of Nicholias.

Para had known the room to be small but with nine people standing there, it felt tiny. Someone said something that Para didn't quite catch and they all sat, Para next to but not in the arms of Petros.

"Para," Petros started "We as a group have a problem and some of the boys think you may be able to help us. Please do not be frightened or upset. If you can help us it would be great, if you cannot then we have lost nothing."

Para was nervous and suddenly felt even more nervous surrounded by eight big men. It briefly went through her head that they were some sort of sect that shared their women. "I would love to help you guys, if I can, you know that."

Petros was allowed to continue as spokesman, it had been part of the deal worked out during the earlier whispered conversations.

"You know already that we take it in turns to guard the winery, to be in charge of security. Para, something very valuable was stolen from the winery and when the CCTV was searched for when it happened it was found that you had visited also. Now, nobody here is accusing you of being involved, we just think you may have seen something that you don't realise could help us find the thief."

"Yes." Para tried not to let her voice shake, "We visited the winery on the round the island trip, but I don't see..."

A voice broke in from the back of the room that Para recognised as Angelos who she didn't quite like but didn't know why. "We want to know why you were on top of the stairs to the top of the vat taking pictures of the office." Angelos had broken the deal that Petros would do the questioning. Para froze.

"I think you know I was taking a photo of my group on the mini bus for my holiday album, I had no interest in the office."

The voice came back from the far side of the room. "So you have never heard of Thierry Jeune or his wife and you have never spent time with them or given them photos of the winery office?"

Para gave a quick "No" that was convincing because it was true although she could see where things were going. She looked at Petros for help.

"Enough Angelos. We are not making accusations here we are asking a friend for help. I suggest that you all carry on with your lines of enquiry now and leave Para and me to enjoy the rest of our evening."

Petros was clearly in charge to the point where the lads all immediately left, even Nicholias, the owner of the house that he was being asked to leave. Para noticed a few of them looking at Angelos with disdain, as if he had spoilt things by speaking out. Angelos was frustrated – he'd explained to his colleagues earlier that he'd tracked what he thought was a lead, to another island, only to be given the slip at the hotel or at the airport. As Para and Petros got ready for bed in silence, Para with a feeling that their conversation was not over, Rebecca and Kitto were thinking about heading towards Rebecca's home that was so much bigger than that of Nicholias.

Kitto thought he had died and gone to heaven. The second bottle of wine arrived as they were getting up to go and Bec carried it with her. The trip to her home Bec made romantically slow. Despite her highest heels, not the best choice over cobbled streets admittedly, she was still much shorter than the excited Kitto and she tucked her shoulder into his armpit. Walking at arms-length had disappeared forever. Arriving at Bec's place they stopped at the door Bec detached herself and turned to face him, with a really concerned look on her face giving Kitto the fear that the night could be ruined and over for some unfathomable reason.

"Oh no, I don't believe it." Her head was thrown back in mock despair. "I cannot for the life of me remember where I put the door key, I should have left someone else in charge of it. I don't suppose you have any ideas Kitto."

He smiled realising the joke, pulled her towards him, wrapped his arms around her waist, his hands in her two back jeans pockets. As Bec's arms encircled Kitto's neck, they kissed deeply and Kitto spent a good five minutes looking through the pockets, massaging the cheeks of her buttocks. Bec could feel herself floating upward as Kitto lifted her with ease and she bent both her legs at the knees, partly in response to his kiss, partly in an attempt to keep her expensive shoes from falling off. Announcing, eventually, that he had discovered the key she found herself being lowered gently down from a foot above the ground and became aware of a passing elderly couple, smiling at them with nostalgia in their eyes.

Opening the door as if it were his own he picked Bec up with ease and she went over his shoulder like a rag doll, giggling like a schoolgirl. Her weight didn't appear to hinder his progress up the stairs and he was even able to talk.

"There'll be no pillaging by the way. Word refers to taking your money and valuables. Sort of, spoils of war. Rape mind, that's a different thing altogether for us Vikings, can't vouch that won't happen."

Rebecca was beginning to wish her bedroom was not right at the top of the house, possibly wearing out her bloke and sapping his energy that she desperately needed to be conserved. Not bothered now about her posh shoes because she was inside her home, she lost one on the first stairs and shook the other one off on a landing where she could see the label that screamed how over-priced the shoes had been, a label that would have meant absolutely nothing to Kitto even if he'd seen it. He gently placed her, on her back, on her own bed and Rebecca knew that she had been in the same position, hours before, spending time getting these tight jeans on. She motioned to remove them but was stopped before she really started.

"Do you imagine a bloke can dream for three years about peeling these jeans off and then not do it when the opportunity arises?" And with that they were peeled off, the pretty lace edged, up the bum, panties that she had very carefully chosen, staying inside them, unseen. Her disappointment though was short lived as Kitto enjoyed kissing the shaved, completely bald area between her legs, completely unaware of how totally different it had looked only hours before. His shirt came off next, much to Rebecca's joy and causing her a small, uncontrolled, intake of breath, and his shirt was quickly followed by her shirt blouse and then her bra, leaving a naked and unusually exposed Rebecca laying there, doing nothing but enjoying the proceedings and pleased that her all over tan revealed no white stodgy bits. Briefly, very briefly, the memory of her first love, Greg, thinking that he had punished her by raping her in her school uniform came to her but was quickly banished from her mind. She had no clue as to when Kitto's bottom half was undressed, her head being in a totally different space by then. In her mind she had imagined, over the last week or so, having him quickly and roughly. Kitto had waited years, would be over excited and would no doubt want things to be as quick as she did. Tonight's talk of mock rape would seal the deal on quick, hard and bouncing off the walls sex.

Except, for the first time in her life Rebecca found that she was in bed with a bloke but she was not in charge. Yes, she had let past boyfriends believe that they had a bit of a say in the matter of timing but this time she was totally incapable of moving and felt very small, fragile and unusually feminine. Kitto was over her, balanced on two knees and two elbows, his stomach a distance above hers. Not only was he perfectly balanced, but he seemed to be stretched into a plank position with his arms reaching out in front of him, his hands holding Rebecca's wrists above her head, on her pillows. A position putting a huge strain on his stomach muscles and impossible to keep up for very long, Rebecca thought as she tried, unsuccessfully, to raise her head enough to see if he had a six pack and what was even lower than that. Giving up, her head flopped back onto the pillow and he started kissing her deeply to the point where she was gasping for air each time he stopped but grateful that as he stretched her body out it gave her the appearance of having a flat stomach. While their tongues fought she attempted to lift her hips off the bed to see if she could have any influence at all on their love making, failed again badly and then cursed that she had never done the sit-ups that she had read about in magazines that would have strengthened her core. Her plank, she decided, would be measured in seconds not minutes and she would have to start to exercise, reading about exercising not really being the same thing.

Paraskevi was in bed watching Petros undress and felt that she should break the awkward silence. "I know he is your friend Petros but there is something about Angelos that worries me and always has done."

Petros turned towards her as he finished undressing but stayed silent and had obviously decided to carry on the conversation in bed, while holding on to the woman that he didn't want to lose.

"Para, I have to tell you a story that you must promise not to repeat to anyone or bring up again." They were both on their backs, Petro's arm around her. "I am telling you this because I trust you and think I know you well." He kissed the top of her head, Para tried to lift herself to face him, Petros held onto her shoulder preferring that they both carry on staring at the ceiling, its wooden beam, the goat bell.

"A year ago we were approached by a person who smuggled people. He suggested to us that there were huge amounts of money to be made for us by smuggling things other than people. He said that we had all the right equipment, there would be no outlay and we would be rich within a year. We had a meeting, the eight of us that oversee the running of the winery – we don't just guard it by the way – and decided we would do it for a year, become rich, then pack it in. There was a lot of discussion over the harm the drugs would do to people and it was explained to us that it would affect no Greeks, the drugs would pass through our country and affect only rich, stupid people. That year is up and bad things have happened. In one of our last deals a Frenchman, the one you were asked if you knew, bought three packages but

242

the idiots in the winery left him alone and he took four. This is how amateur and trusting we are. Also Angelos ended up being the weakest of the eight of us and has tried the drug himself. He wont admit that he is now addicted but some of the boys say he is. Finally, and worst of all the people who use us to help transport their evil filth have said no to us stopping, have said that if we stop now they will go to the authorities." Petros stopped, carried on staring at the ceiling, waited for his confession to permeate Paraskevi's brain.

Kitto had one hundred per cent control of Rebecca and she was forced to lay back and accept what was coming to her. As she opened her eyes to see if he was having equal enjoyment, she saw his head close to hers, smiling as if he knew he controlled her and enjoyed the power he had over her. With anyone else it would have panicked her but Kitto was sweet and thoughtful so she closed her eyes again, smiled, bit her lower lip and lay back to enjoy whatever happened.

Eventually she could feel her orgasm approaching and whispered to Kitto to climax the two of them together and was shocked when he stopped, slipped out of her and started again from scratch. She found herself moaning and whimpering, feeling that talk would spoil the moment and determined that she would not beg him.

Paraskevi eventually spoke after much thought. "I think I may have been tempted with stories of riches as well." She said it to make Petros feel better but both of them knew it wasn't true. "I must be frank with you also."

Glad to be looking upward now, not at Petros, she continued. "Rebecca and I came to this island to find the drug runners. I am, as I truthfully told you, a taverna owner with my family, I also look after Rebecca's very expensive villa on my island, she has a few places that she owns. Rebecca is not police but from what I can work out, she gets information that she sells to the police. The Frenchman that Angelos mentioned, Rebecca is chasing to France and will get evidence of him and sell it to the police. I have his address in my head if you want it. Rebecca has promised me, and I believe her that before anything is said to the police, she will let me know and I can get you away from the winery. I am sorry."

Petros received, gladly, the address of Thierry Jeune from Para and, the next morning, got that information to Angelos. They all thought Angelos mad but at least he had the will to get back the missing heroin or the money obtained for it. He would probably travel to France in pursuit of Jeune and return with the money to be split eight ways.

"The bastards teasing me" Rebecca thought and knowing he wasn't into football, wondered if he was thinking about philosophy to keep himself going. The next time he brought her almost to climax and stopped, her feelings were more concentrated and more frustrating, the third time it happened she realised that he wasn't thinking about anything other than her. He was concentrating on her and her feelings rather than himself and, for Rebecca, this was a totally new concept. If men were from Mars, she thought, and women were from Venus, then perhaps Kitto was from the planet Pluto. I've never before met a Plutonian, where has this Plutonian been all my life, was the thought racing through her head until she tried to analyse what she had just thought and realised that her brain waves had been hijacked, hormones and endorphins were coursing through her body, slowly turning her into a mindless jelly.

The fourth time he teased her she screamed at him "Kitto, if you don't finish me this time I'll...I'll" she searched desperately for something horrible to threaten him with "I'll drill a hole in the bottom of your fishing boat!" She had given in, she had begged.

It seemed to do the trick; Bec screamed like never before and didn't care if the neighbours heard as she wanted the whole world to hear. They climaxed together and her whole body shook. As he let go of her wrists, feeling came back into her hands and she thrust her six hour old finger nails deeply into his shoulder muscles without him seeming to notice.

Petros let go of Para's shoulder and they faced each other. Petros took the lead. "Shit. What are we going to do? The boring window painter and the boring taverna worker just want to be boring again, to live a boring life together." That sentence would stay with Para forever, it was huge. It said he wanted to get out. It said he assumed she wanted to get out. It said he still wanted their relationship to continue. It said he wanted a life that he had described as 'together'. It also asked her if she wanted the same, without asking the question. The couple slept on it holding each other tightly knowing that in the morning they would still be holding each other tightly and that decisions would have to be made.

Bec's head was scrambled, her body sweated, her chest still heaved with heavy breathing and he could feel her bubbling inside. "Your crying" he whispered to her "let me know when we can talk and I'll shut up and just look at your body until then, especially this curvy bit between your waist and your hips." He started to move his lips from one of her closed eyes to the other, and back, kissing her tears, the salt water taste being very familiar to him, a fisherman.

Rebecca eventually recovered and wondered at the amount of times blokes had rolled their heavy, sweaty bodies off her and fallen asleep and, the one time she is totally incapacitated, this bloke was still hovering over her and wanted to know when she would be able to have a conversation.

"What d'you want to talk about then" she managed to get out after a couple of minutes, opening her eyes at the same time.

"Not sure really" Kitto hesitated and started probing again, trying to keep her going but stopping when she took hold of him and moved his now very non-erect member away from her, wanting that conversation.

Kitto moved off her, lay by her side, effortlessly picked up her body, making Rebecca feel like a rag doll again and he placed her on top of him, her head on his chest his one hand back on her buttock where it had all started with the key, the other hand playing with the back of her neck and hair.

"I'm scared, very scared." Kitto started "Don't get me wrong, tonight was all my dreams come true at once but I can't help worrying, what if this was temporary and we ruined the friendship we had. I'm confused. If I had been given the choice, would I have chosen tonight and no friendship, or just carry on the friendship? Do you see this as a one off Bec?"

She had been concentrating on his fast heartbeat, millimetres from her ear pressed into his chest. The beating was slowing down gradually, while her fingers played with the long sweaty hairs on his chest and thinking as he spoke. Her immediate answer made no sense. "Plutonian man wanting commitment from a woman?"

"Sorry"

"Nothing, scrambled brain, ignore me."

Knowing now definitely how Kitto felt about her made it easier for her to be totally honest as she lifted her head to face him and to look him in the eye to show how serious she was.

"I don't do one-offs Kitto. This was no spur of the moment thing for me. I've thought about this for weeks. This is the way I see things going forward from tonight, you tell me if you agree or not and I will accept whatever you say. This is not me being controlling mind you, this is me telling you how I feel to see if you feel the same. First off, the way I see it, we are no longer just good friends we are a couple, we are lovers and we let everyone know that."

Kitto dived in, "No need to tell anyone in St. Ives or the surrounding area, due to that open window they probably just heard you howling like a wolf and put two and two together. I figure we're the talk of all the pubs in St. Ives by now."

There was pride in Kitto's voice, pride on knowing he'd caused that howling through being in control, totally. Rebecca blushed slightly, accepting her passive role, totally willing to give herself, to be dominated, to have someone else make all the decisions, well some of them anyway. Still smiling she focused her brain and continued.

"From now on until the end of our relationship, whenever that be and if it does actually end, I do not look at another man and, as you are fully aware, I have been hurt so many times that if you as much as glance at anything female, human or non-human I will cut your balls off. One more thing before you say yes or no, in our relationship I want you to be in charge of my body. You obviously know it better than I do, please do to it whatever you want, whenever you want. Let me tell you that if you carry on doing to me what you just did then it definitely won't be me ending our relationship."

Kitto looked pensive "Can I think about it?" He joked and then protected himself from the punches thrown by his lover. Swatting each punch easily, the fight turned into a wrestling match. During mock fighting she noticed the cuts from her nails in his shoulders, the cuts that branded him as having had a recent lover, and that said to any other woman "taken, back off."

"Do one thing for me Kitto, please"

"Anything"

"Stay with me tonight, wake with me in the morning, just be here."

Kitto did not have to work out the maths of missing the money from a fishing session; it was the furthest thing from his mind.

Chapter 18

Marc loved the room he was in. It felt oddly familiar and reminded him of his grandmother. The old couple, Marcel and Gabrielle Bourbeau, had modernised their wine making, as far as they thought it needed to be modernised, but had kept their cottage looking as it had looked when they'd been in their thirties. Marc had suggested to them, long ago, that bringing electricity into the barn meant that they could have it in their cottage also but they could see no need, no advantage to be gained. He was well over six feet tall and his imposing beard was designed to give the impression that he was different to other people, a class above others when it came to wine; the authority in the region when it came to what wine was average, what was good and how to turn the average into good.

He'd recently seen the starkness of this room, with its worn furniture, in daylight but tonight, the gaslight from the wall fitting combined with the glow from the fire, used still for cooking, gave the furniture softened edges. Any colours in the room were muted by soft light or shadow. The group sat around the hub of the cottage, the table of the living and kitchen area, their arms and hands aware of the cut marks in the table block from a century of cleaning fish and game but in the knowledge that Gabrielle had scrubbed the table so hard, a million times, that the ammonia smell was still creeping out of the grain of the wood. Marc sat at the head as Gabrielle was nervous and insisted on sitting close to Marcel on one of the longer table sides. Opposite them, standing out as if she were a gold sovereign amongst a pile of copper coinage was Laurette Brochard, niece of Gabrielle and the last remaining member of the family alive. The bright and youthful colours that she wore and the apparent softness of her extremely made-up face, combined with her designer briefcase that had travelled miles on the Paris Metro, in fact, everything about her clashed with her surroundings and she felt, very much, as if she didn't fit in.

"I suppose the first thing to say..." Marc opened the conversation, his mouth moving the large beard, the grey hairs picking up the light and sparkling "...is that we are not here to make any decisions. We are here to discuss things so that Gabrielle and Marcel can think about things before making any decisions at a later date and you, Laurette, can think about things also. I have been speaking on the phone to Laurette at her office in Paris and it is a bit confusing for her to suddenly be told that her mother's sister lives here and makes wine. I understand that the sisters lost touch some years back." Laurette, nods, looks at Gabrielle who also nods. If there is a long story there then the only thing that all the participants will learn of it is two nods and silence.

"Laurette does remember, vaguely, visiting here when she was very young but cannot remember the wine making, only the farm. I wonder if she visited in the height of summer when activity in the vineyard was both low and slow.

Laurette, I have explained to you that your auntie and uncle want to leave the vineyard to you in their will, that they would hope that you have the energy to modernise the wine making process here, they would like the responsibility of the running of things and also the hard work involved to be taken off their shoulders as soon as possible but they also need their security through their later years."

Laurette, although feeling uncomfortably out of place in the room, was used to meetings, used to gap searching and used to knowing when to listen and when to speak. She felt it was time to explain her situation and turned her head from Marc to Gabrielle.

"Yes, I am, of course, thrilled and honoured that you have included me in your will and that your beautiful vineyard and cottage will remain in our family. I am praying that you both have many years left in you so that I can still enjoy my lifestyle in Paris, maybe visit for weekends and holidays to learn the processes and to take over eventually at the end of your long and happy lives."

Marc had already discussed this with Marcel and Gabrielle. They all knew that running a vineyard and winery was not learnt through treating it as a weekend hobby, that Laurette would be 'clubbing it' in Paris for a good few years yet. Gabrielle knew that Marc had a plan and looked to him now to speak on her behalf.

"We have devised a plan of the future Laurette, a plan that we think will benefit all of us around this table. A plan that we want to put to you to see if it is as beneficial to your plans as we think it is to the three of us. If you agree then it will involve lawyers and contracts but let me try and explain simply before they get involved and complicate things to boost their fees.

At the moment I look after a vineyard owned by a British woman who very rarely comes here. I organise the planting of new vines, merlot mainly, decide the times to spray, the date of harvest of each parcel of vines, organise the gangs of pickers from abroad, the blending of the various wines made from each grape and each parcel of land, the tasting by the local government officials, bottling, labelling, everything. I have, over many years, brought that wine from a generic 'produce of France' to a better 'produce of Bergerac' and am now fighting this year for them to be labelled

'Pecharmant' as I believe the wine is now distinctive enough. Of course this makes the wine more valuable, it gets a better price if, and it's a big if, the Pecharmant board agree with me.

As we all age, me included, I believe my vocation is in improving all the wines of this village or even our commune, what will eventually be your vineyard included. I have yet to speak to the British woman but will suggest to her that she employs a general manager to do most of the things that I have just described and that she employs me as an advisor on when to spray, pick and make the wine and how to blend. Of course, the more vineyards I advise, the more I can produce good wines from our area that are distinctive to the Pecharmant region and will therefore command a higher price. The vineyard you will one day inherit has some old vines that make an extremely heavy and traditional wine. It sells but, to move with the times, it is best to imitate the wines of Bordeaux, down the river, but still keeping the distinctive grape of this region. This is why I have slowly changed variety ratios at the British woman's vineyard and would wish to do the same here."

Marc had become too technical for Laurette and knew it. She was a city woman and he was guessing that for Laurette, wine came not from the field but from the supermarket and she bought on price not quality. A cheap bottle for everyday drinking, but splashing out on an over priced bottle for a special occasion, he guessed. In his mind, all Parisians ordered the second lowest priced wine on the menu.

"Our suggestion is as follows; the three of you form a company and each of you has equal shares. You employ me as an advisor and we get in a general manager to take the strain off Marcel and Gabrielle. Of course if you had any outlandish ideas, Laurette, then you could be outvoted by their combined votes. Marcel and Gabrielle would leave, in their wills their shares to each other and, in the event of the death of the surviving shareholder the shares would go to you.

Put simply, you would have 33% of the company; they would hold 67% and they would have the final say on all decisions and the guarantee of living the rest of their lives in this cottage. In the event of the death of one of these lovely people their partner would inherit their shares and they would still have overall control. On the death of the other partner you would inherit and hold 100% and full control. The inheritance taxes implications are not clear within a company setup hence the need for lawyers and contracts. What are your first impressions?"

Laurette was impressed.

"I love the idea. It seems to me that I can stay in Paris, enjoy my youth while I have it and look forward to a life down here in later life. I know you all think I am too young at the moment to take something like this on in a serious way, it is an impression that I have not tried to hide but I would like to show you that there is a mature side to me if you would allow. Once I receive my 33% share of the company then I assume that I would be entitled to a salary based on a third of the profits. This I would probably blow in Paris on fine food and wine. A few weeks ago, before Marc rang me, I had no idea that I could hold any shares in a vineyard and so, if I didn't have the profits then, I would not miss what I wasn't expecting, if that makes sense. I suggest to you that it is written into my contract that my share of profits be reinvested in the company. I would not be losing out as I would be adding to a company that I would one day have full control of."

In unison both Gabrielle and Marcel pushed themselves back into their chairs smiling, Gabrielle with a small tear in her eye seeing herself, many years ago, in Laurette's sensible attitude. They both looked at Marc nodding their heads to say yes, please proceed; we have made the right decision. As Marc stood to shake hands with Marcel they both smiled broadly to see Gabrielle and Laurette hugging.

On the same night another French family were not hugging. They were cramped into a car too small for them and the wife was insistent. "This is stupid. I know you are being macho and taking the lion's share of the driving but it makes sense for me to drive tonight and you join your sons to sleep in the back seat. It means we'll eventually get home quicker, we can unpack and you can get rid of your stuff to wherever you are taking it. The quicker it is away from us the better. Did you change the skins by the way?"

Thierry Jeune was trying to take in what his wife was saying in English, translate it into French, to concentrate on the road and to translate his answer from his native French back into English to be able to reply."

"Sorry, I thought I'd said. Before we got to the border to leave Italy I used gloves to remove the wine from three of the Greek boxes and got the flatpack Italian boxes out and put the wine in there. I even had a conversation rehearsed for customs where we would joke with them about taking Italian merlot to France because they make it better than us, the other box being from our holiday in Greece. But you are right, I'll stop at the next services to swap with you and grab some sleep if you are sure you are ok to drive."

Kitto was holding Rebecca as if she would float away like a helium filled balloon if he let go. He knew that his lover was desperate to change her bed sheets but had said that she wouldn't until he was gone. He loved lying, staring at the ceiling, and he enjoyed playing with the back of her neck as much as she enjoyed him doing it. Kitto hadn't worked for days and that made him feel guilty. They had gone through the whole of Pel's take away menu, had playfully argued each time about whose turn it was to collect the food, and now it was surely time to start looking towards getting back to reality.

"Bec, I'm going to have to get back to work at some point. I can't lie here and watch you spending out on everything every day, it don't seem natural."

"If you say so my lover. I want to be by your side every minute of every day but I won't go on that boat with you to have you throw wet fish at me again. I have to go to France tomorrow to see a client but should get back to you after a couple of days. We both need to work out how we can be together because for the next couple of days in France I am going to ache for you."

Rebecca's going away present was as she hoped it would be and as it was then Kitto's turn to pick up the takeaway Rebecca sat up in bed and made flight, train and car hire arrangements to get her to her French vineyard. Once done she put her phone down, breathed out a sigh and stared at the wall in deep thought.

I am controlling this situation in front of me only because I have the money, I have the property, I have the means to give us a future. Us. For the first time since Greg, my first ever lover, I am trying to be controlling for us not me. I am not controlling the people around me for my sole benefit, I am working for two, for us. I am trying my hardest to let Kitto dictate the little things in life, trying hard to leave him in his squaller because he loves the smell of us in the bed but if he doesn't let me change these bed sheets soon! You can do it Rebecca. You can climb into a cold damp bed each time because he wants you to and you want him to have his say and – no you are not going to spill your coffee so that the sheets have to be swapped out for clean. Behave.

Chapter 19

The hire car crunched on the gravel of the drive of Rebecca's Bergerac vineyard home, the place she called "The Chateau" which was a name, far too grand for its English country cottage looks. She found the key in its usual spot, at the bottom of a pot in the shed of the small back garden, and was soon in her living room and thinking of unpacking.

Somewhere in this house were the paper versions of some of her earlier poetry, always written out on paper, and hopefully the one she had remembered from when she and James had come to France to pick grapes and have a good time.

Settled in an armchair she rang Paraskevi.

"Hi, Para, it's Bec, I have a weird question for you."

"Your questions are always weird, especially in Greek, best you keep to English for now." Para giggled, pleased to hear from her friend.

"Para, Kitto's friends, all those hunky guys you went out with each night, do you remember if any of them had very blue, penetrating eyes?"

"No, I don't think you should, blue doesn't suit you, especially in a dress."

"Sorry!"

"I see you more in pastel shades. I take it you received the wedding invite then?"

"Para, have you been on the wine? What dress? What wedding?"

"I am away from the taverna now, away from ears, I have to get tomatoes ready for tonight."

"Slowly for me Para, I have been travelling. Blue eyes, dress, wedding, tomatoes?"

Para took in a deep breath wondering where to begin.

"Bec I have been struggling in my head. Whether to keep quiet about everything and hope it all goes away or to tell you everything so you are safe but maybe my life is ruined forever."

"Para, you're not making much sense. Can you start at the beginning and try not to panic?"

"Okay. You left our holiday island. Pedro and me (I call him Pedro now) we moved to the hotel you paid for. We didn't like the beds – it is another story. I find out from Pedro that the Frenchman you follow he pays for three boxes, somehow he takes four, they watch all the CCTV to see what happens and, hey presto, someone sees me at the top of a ladder on the side of a vat, taking pictures of the office. I make sense so far?"

Rebecca is scared, for herself and for Para.

"Para are you okay? I had no idea the guards knew about the wine boxes of drugs."

"I am fired lots of questions at me but it gives me a lot of answers also. By the questions of eight men I find out that they are not the guards only, they are organising the wine boxes but they tell me that they do it for one year only to make lots of money then they stop. They say that year almost up so they stop now.

My English is down the toilet since you left me, do you think?"

"Para, did they hurt you? Did Petros get angry?"

"No, it was all really friendly and calm. I told Pedro about you and you would go to the police but you would tell me first and I would save Pedro. That you promised me. They each had their money and are now on various little Greek islands or gone to Australia and one to America. Do not ask me who went where, I wouldn't tell you even if I knew, and I don't.

Oh, yes, the blue eyes, they all went away happy except for the boy called Angelos who, Pedro told me, they think he has foolishly been using some of the heroin. He is angry about the Frenchman thieving box number four and he left the island without telling anyone where he is going. Possibly to France to try to get his money back. Para, he has blue eyes, very penetrating as you said they were. You think they are sexy?"

"Maybe under different circumstances. He came to my holiday hotel and scared me but I managed to lose him at the airport, on my way back home. Tell me Para, if the boys have all gone to different places then who is running the winery."

"The Turkish men who started this all off have brought in a winery team from Turkey who are willing to do their dirty work just to be in Europe. It is good that you lost Angelos, I do not like him, he is no angel. So you are home now but with no invitation?"

"Right, forget blue eyes. What is all this about a wedding. I take it that Petros, I mean Pedro, was not angry with you then."

"Well, I will be quick as I have the tomatoes now and I am headed back to the taverna. We are still madly in love and want to marry. I have a taverna, eventually, Pedro has money to put removable plastic sides and a plastic permanent roof on the taverna so we are a perfect match. He has taken his mother's surname that he will give to me (that story is way too complicated for now) and my mother loves him and bosses him around her kitchen like the son she always wanted. I serve with my father who was angry about the shame of the family of Yiorgo to who I was engaged, but thought it was okay when he suddenly found out about Pedro's money. Does that fill you in?"

"Wow, I feel like I've been away for months, not days. You have been busy. And you say you've sent me a wedding invite. Did it say Rebecca and guest, as I too have hitched up. His name is Kitto."

"His?"

"Yes his, what do you mean, his?"

"Bec I think it is wonderful that you have found a man to change you from gay and stop you being lesvian."

"This phone call gets stranger by the minute. What on earth makes you think I'm gay? Anyway it's lesbian not lesvian." The agreement they have to correct each other coming at a strange moment in the conversation.

"Well a number of things. Mainly the way you were looking at me when we swam naked in your pool. You were looking at my boobs and between my legs and smiling. After that, I thought you noticed that I showered only when you were out, if I could, or dressed in the bathroom, and slept away from the hotel. Mainly though, after I met Pedro you had a choice of seven young men served on a plate for you and chose to stay at home. All the time you go on about hating men. When Pedro's friends asked about where you were, when I first met Pedro, I told them you were gay. I slapped Pedro when he asked if he could come to bed with both of us. Also in Greek we pronounce your b as a v so we say a lesvian from the island of Lesvos, not Lesbos."

Rebecca's mind is racing and she cannot disagree with anything that Para has said so sticks first to grammar.

"I will explain better when I see you at your wedding but for now accept that it is the difference between ancient Greek and Modern Greek. We write the island of Lesbos but pronounce it Lesvos but we always say and write lesbian and, by the way, I have never been with a woman. As I said his name is Kitto, he is from my village in Cornwall and he is a big, hunky fisherman."

"So you will never go hungry, for food or sex." Para was giggling like a schoolgirl.

Bec was broken out of the spell by a knock on the door and explained to Para who was near her taverna anyway and they agreed to speak later.

"Marc, how are you It's been too long. Are your children – our vines doing well? Come in."

Marc was surprised to see Rebecca having not seen her in France for so long. It was coincidental timing and he had noticed her hire car in the drive. He sat and explained his plans for his future and his hopes for the future wines of their commune. He was concerned that he might be dropping Rebecca in it with nobody to look after the day to day work at the vineyard.

"Look, if this is all a bit sudden then I can make changes slowly and change my position slowly. I know a few people who could run the business day to day and I could arrange interviews to see if you can get on with any of them."

Rebecca listened and her crowded mind, not recovered from the many conversations with Para, wondered if Marc had ever spoken to a deaf person, lip reading through his beard being impossible.

"Marc, I love the way this is going, I think. Leave the interviews for a bit. Go away and have a think about this. If I hire you as a consultant only, as you suggest, how long would I have to hire you for as a teacher – to teach viticulture and viniculture to a Cornish fisherman?"

Marc left a happy man. If he could charge a fee to teach a fisherman to run a vineyard and winery while he built up his client base for his new business as an advisor, then there would not be the expected drop in salary that he'd been dreading.

Rebecca too was happy and started to rummage through the desk draws of her office looking for the old brown folder with old poems in.

She found the folder and had to go through the sheets of paper twice before finding the one that had sparked her memory when St. Emilion was first mentioned. Reading through the poem gave a slightly different feel to what she had remembered writing but it did give a feel for the care-free time she had spent with James.

Wandering old quarter streets
tall built narrow ways with
soft coloured sun scorched render
pastel paint stripped shutters
blue house numbers to blue street names
holding each other we strolled
in search of antidote to hunger
and lack of red wine's tannic tongue
when sudden rain cooled down on us.

Giant drops of razor wire
globules rested on parched cobbles
dust swimming on aqua globes

no haste, we slowly cared for nought
natures way to clean and cool.

Drenched sleeves
of cheesecloth shirts, we found
the smallest cafe step
staff rubbing us with rough towels, laughing
apologised their countries weather
specs tissued and returned
the seated locals muttering idiot tourist words.

Rebecca dreamed of James that night and woke
in a sweat. Reading for half an hour calmed her
brain so that she could sleep again but only up to
the dream point where Kitto walked in on
Rebecca and Paraskevi in bed together and asked
if he should shoot them or join them and waited
while they looked at each other, both women
waiting for the other to answer.

Rising early, just before dawn, she was soon on
the road to St. Emilion, soon at the address she
had for the Jeune family and where she had
expected a long wait and soon, staring in horror at
the sight in front of her.

Chapter 20

"Merde, I've lost him."

Rebecca was about to move out to the next lane, to accelerate down the road, to try and catch Jeune's car again when, at the last minute, she saw the flash of blue against white, the blue door of Jeune's car pulling off the road and into the services. Swerving back into the right hand lane she followed his lead to the right, pulled into the car parking area two cars behind him and parked her hire car four rows behind him.

She had travelled to St. Emilion expecting to have to wait from morning till night for the Jeune's to arrive home from their holiday but the swines had shared the driving and got back early. This was a mistake by Rebecca, her mind not fully on the job or her calculations. Curse Kitto. She watched them unpack the car that was old, white but with a replacement door in blue from an earlier crash and that made it stand out. Jeune repacked four boxes of wine into the boot and she had followed him for hours to a Paris flat, with goons guarding outside it, on guard. She had a photo of the block that he went into and a photo of his hand on the top-but-one door buzzer with the flat number next to it, but there was no way she was going to get any closer to any action or even get out of her car. As far as Geordie would be concerned that was it, there would be no reason to carry on with the surveillance. But she had. She had carried on. Despite her weariness, her tiredness, she did retrace the route back towards St. Emilion, following Jeune's car.

Jeune jumped, hurriedly, from the car and ran towards the services, clicking locked his car from about five metres away but then hurriedly returning to ensure that the boot was locked and Rebecca knew instantly that he had not peed since leaving home, needed to empty his over-excited bladder and was probably too scared to use the toilet of the Paris drug barons. She had a similar need to pee but had to ignore it. Now was the chance to change her life for ever. The tight leather gloves that she put on would have to be a weird fashion statement as they did not match well with her large sunglasses. Her mini rucksack that she grabbed from the passenger seat and threw over her left shoulder, cracked down heavily on her hip bone letting her know that her French pistol, larger than the Cretan pistol, had found its way to the bottom of the bag. The key, made by Pierre was making an impression in her back jeans pocket and made her think, briefly, of Kitto. If Jeune had been able to lock the car while moving away from it then the key she had copied, with no battery, had indeed been the family spare. She took a deep breath in and walked towards the services, rubbing up against Jeune's car as she went.

At his car she stopped briefly, heard and felt her heart beating fast, looked in and walked away from the car quickly. The French over reaction of throwing her hands in the air with her head thrown back was well practiced and she might as well have shouted to anyone watching that she had left something in Jeune's car. She turned. Approaching Jeune's car, the blood was pumping through her neck and making her feel dizzy. She placed the key in the blue passenger side door and listened. Nothing. She moved quickly to the driver's side door calling herself an idiot as she moved. Clunk. "Pierre, you are beautiful, you are a master."

Quickly she moved to the boot, it opened, she took the maroon leather briefcase and noticed that it had once belonged to a rich Arabian with five names, there being five Arabic symbols embossed on the case. It fitted neatly under her jacket, away from view and the car doors were re-locked. She walked towards the services, her need for a pee now probably greater than Jeune's had been.

Nerves supplied more than just a pee and, finding the case locked, she used the penknife in her bag to cut through the leather bottom of the bag, away from the combination locks. The notes, all in high denomination Euros, were not in bundles and would have been impossible to count quickly. Jeune had foolishly taken the amount on trust. It took seconds to carefully transfer the money to her rucksack without dropping any to the toilet floor, that was for all but the last few notes that she used, as some sort of symbolic gesture, to wipe her backside with and then stuffed the briefcase down behind the toilet pan for the cleaners to find and be upset that the bag was cut and their find useless. Her jeans back up to her waist and the pockets checked for sets of car keys, her rucksack could not now leave her and sat properly, both straps used, on her back.

Walking back to her car Rebecca physically realised the fact that her heart beat had dropped slightly and that the sensation of wiping her bum with Euros using a gloved hand, may never leave her. She didn't get all the way back to the car however, her attention caught by a fight, probably caused through road rage, between two men with a small crowd gathering around them, some obscenely videoing the fight on their phones hoping that something funny would happen that they could upload to the internet. It was near her car so she walked quite close to the action and her head shot back to her school days;-

Greg and Ross fighting over me in the school playground with kids cheering around them, me not knowing whether I should watch, walk away, or try and stop it. My horror as kicks found their target. Lucy Watson screaming at me "Come on

Becca, shout for your Greg" but Lucy Watson's
life wasn't complicated like mine; she didn't know
about Ross.

The car park fighters were shouting at each
other in English but with accents. Fists were flying
but very few making contact. They wanted to shout
at each other more than hurt each other but the
shouting had over boiled. Had one cut the other
up on the motorway? Why had they both come
into the services?

I had instigated their fight without wanting it to
go that far. My first physical lover, Greg who had
been so exciting and new, was getting boring and
samey in his loving and I tried to control the
situation and make him jealous to perk things up
but I would never have wanted it to go this far.
Would they ever be friends again?

One man switched from English to French to
perhaps gain the support of the crowd and
Rebecca suddenly realised that it was Jeune. She
should have fled, there and then but found herself
transfixed, watching and remembering the school
playground and trying hard to separate the two
things.

Can't remember how me and Ross ended up
alone but it was me that instigated the snog and
then, in for a penny..."Oi you, get off me baps."

274

"I haven't touched your baps."

I just smiled at him and my school jumper looked like a bag of ferrets for a while and I giggled wildly but I stopped him when he tried to go downstairs. I was not going to be called a slag by anyone.

Greek from the other fighter. "Shit, it's blue eyes." This was spoken out loud and now it really was time for her to go but she was frozen to the spot, caught between past and present.

I wanted control of the situation. I wanted control of Greg, I knew I could change him, to make him be the way I wanted him to be. I wanted that early passion back, the time when he couldn't leave me alone, I wanted him to be jealous so I told him Ross and me had a fling and it was all my fault, not to blame Ross. He demanded every little detail. Went on and on about every detail. Was he getting off on listening to me telling him? Was I getting off by telling him?

Two lorry drivers, distinctive in their working blues, pulled the fighters apart quite easily, like dogs being placed back on their leads and the crowd started to part as the school bell went – except it wasn't a school bell it was the fire alarm in the services and people were rushing out through the main doors. Cars were heading too

quickly for the exit and getting into a jam. Panic.
Horns blowing.

*The school bell rang for the afternoon lessons
and Greg and Ross parted as if it had been pre-
arranged that they would stop on the bell. The
kids around them groaned at the end of their
excitement and I stood looking at Greg trying to
work out where the blood was coming from. Ross
walked off to lessons but Greg came to me looking
at the ground avoiding my eyes, I went to feel his
face where the blood was but he pushed my hand
away. My school bag over my left shoulder, he
grabbed me by the right wrist and marched us both
towards the school gate. My parents were never
home during the day, too busy nurturing other
people's kids and I knew Greg was taking me
there, I knew he would bed me all afternoon,
reclaim me, I worried about getting his blood on
my bedsheets but thrilled that he would not be his
boring self and I was in for an exciting time.*

The police arrived in what seemed a typical
French over-reaction to the fight or was it perhaps
in response to the fire alarm? Rebecca walked
calmly to her car and went to get in. A woman,
running to her own car shouted to Rebecca, in
French, to hurry. "They have planted a bomb in
the toilets with a message in Arabic on the bomb."
Rebecca started her engine, joined the jam heading
for the exit and prayed that she would not end up

276

anywhere near blue eyes or his car. Her head was spinning; CCTV would be searched for the bomber, good that she'd worn gloves, bad that she'd entered the services with a briefcase under her coat.

We didn't go the road way to my house, we went through the woods at the back of the school. I started saying "No Greg, please no" but he knew I didn't really mean it. I could have sat down and stopped the whole thing but I slowed, waited for him to pull me and then took three quick steps to catch up with him. He was acting the macho boss but I knew I had controlled the whole thing and was still in control although it wouldn't have looked like that to an onlooker. When he found a spot in the woods that he liked for the two of us he threw me down onto my back, stood looking at me for a few seconds while I tried to look scared, just for him, and told him I was sorry and then he came down to me.

The road was pretty clear after finally exiting the services. Who cared where Jeune was, who cared where blue eyes was. The money was in the back of her car, one glove was jettisoned near the next motorway exit, the other glove shortly after. The car key was kept as a keepsake. Surely, when it was discovered that the so-called bomb was a briefcase with the bottom ripped out of it, there would be no need for further investigation.

I was meant to feel the shock that he'd planned. I'd read the bodice ripper that Janice had lent me, her first explaining to me what bodice ripper meant, and now I was in the book and playing the feeble woman with my man and loving it. I gently held the back of his head as...

The adrenaline from the fight was still in him and needed to come out.

The adrenaline from the fight was coming out through his eyes and through his barking animal-like groans.

The adrenaline from the fight pumped into me and he exploded in less than a minute "You bastard" he shouted as he came and then flopped down, lifeless, on top of me. I held his head and looked forward to role playing out this scene many times in the comfort of a bed in the future. I had controlled a situation where our sex life would be more exciting.

He was crying "I'm sorry, I'm sorry, I shouldn't have done that."

I probably went too far with "It's ok Greg, I probably deserved it."

Yes, it was a total shock when he got up and walked away without walking me home but I thought our parting was temporary, that it was part of my punishment.

"Shit again" a loud car horn, a long blast of someone leaning on a horn. Rebecca was in two lanes, white lining and wandering out of control. "Where the hell am I? How long have I been driving? Thank God I'm on the right hand carriageway. Look at the state of me I need to get home and now." Rebecca's body was trembling, her hands shaking the steering wheel. Her heart pounding like never before but she couldn't work out whether it was from the horn blast, or from memories of Greg, or both?

She apologised to the car behind after making sure it wasn't blue eyes. The last thing on Earth that she wanted was to be stopped by the police with a bag in the back of her car containing a gun and a large amount of money. A sign loomed large up ahead, explaining her situation to her. She had gone too far down the road, would have to come off at the next junction and retrace her steps, her clothes were damp from her daydream and she had been crying without knowing it. Inwardly she apologised to Kitto and wondered if the exciting dream of a schoolgirl romance had broken a promise to him.

That was the end of me and Greg. He didn't tell me it was over, just never called, never answered my messages, always avoided me. Ross was interested but I wasn't. Found myself what Mam called "A nice little boy" who was obedient, took me where I wanted to go, spent all his money on me and was completely boring. Half way through that relationship I met up with Greg, secretly. We talked. He told me how it could never be the same after, what he said was his shameful rape. He seemed to think that I had nothing to do with it and I was merely the victim of his uncontrolled anger. He thanked me for not reporting him to the police and we tried kissing even though we were both seeing someone else. He was right there was no passion left in the kiss, we had expended it all on that afternoon and it was at exactly that point in my life that I determined to control everything around me, to be completely in charge but to spend weeks planning and thinking things through before taking any actions. I did not want another failure like Greg but then, I don't suppose we went out on a whimper.

The last part of her journey was a casual and slow drive towards her French home. It was dusk, as she parked her car and eerily quiet. It always disturbed her that the French countryside was so quiet, so devoid of life, a ghostly tribute to the fact that the race that she sometimes lived amongst seemed to shoot and eat almost everything that moved.

Chapter 21

Rebecca visited her downstairs cellar and brought up a bottle of the red from the first year that Marc had started improving their wine, it was needed to help her to sleep later. She called it 'their' wine because the deal was that Rebecca did nothing except own the vineyard; Marc did everything for fifty percent of the profits and Rebecca took the other fifty percent in a mixture of wine and money. Of course this was all calculated after taking out money for reinvestment in better vines and more modern plant and on that point there had to be total trust of Marc's efforts.

She went to the kitchen area and could see, from the doorway, the irons in the original black grate of the kitchen fireplace. The irons were all upright in a brass cylinder that suited the black grate but clashed with the rest of the kitchen that was made up of separate units in varnished wood but in a modern style that pretended to be old. She closed the curtains from the dark, switched on the lamp of the cooker hood, poured herself a glass of wine, took a candle from a drawer and lit it. Out of the brass cylinder she pulled a four pronged fork that had one prong snapped off. On one side of the old fireplace was an oven, the other side had a water boiler with a brass tap but Rebecca went to the cast iron door of the cupboard above the fireplace where food used to be kept warm in the chimney breast, the cupboard being set into the brickwork. Into the cupboard she placed a lighted candle so that she could see the three holes towards the back of the cupboard and in its ceiling. The three prongs of the fork in her hand fitted neatly into the three holes and the click meant that the wall of the rear of the oven opened to reveal the combination lock on the door of her safe. On her phone contacts, the mobile number for "French Safety Corporation" gave her the not very memorable combination.

Rather than place into the safe, what she would later refer to as the Jeune money, she instead extracted all the Euros that were already in there, the whole were now on the kitchen table, the only original piece of furniture in the house and Rebecca had a ghostly flash through her mind of long ago family monies earned by past occupants of her cottage and presented to the woman of the house to keep the family going. The amounts here were more than this ancient table had seen before and setting up her laptop she started a spreadsheet and made a more modern table. Laboriously she counted the Euros from the safe. Even more laboriously she counted the Jeune money. Both figures were added to the spreadsheet. She entered into the modern computer table the amount she knew was in her safe in St. Ives and in the safe at her Greek villa. Next she added the known value of her four storey home in St. Ives and the amount that she originally paid for her Greek villa – she assumed no profit from a sale even though she had paid only half its true value.

These figures were totalled and then halved as if to be shared by two people. She had in her mind a figure that it would take for one person to live very comfortably for a year in France assuming no profit from the vineyard, any profit would be a wonderful bonus. She set up a number of cells with mini formulae that took her 'comfortable living for a year' figure and divided it into her total pot and a second cell that added the result to her age and that gave the answer that her and Kitto could live comfortably until they were one hundred and twenty nine.

That assumed a lot with regard to Kitto and his plans for the rest of his life, something that she couldn't control and didn't want to control. His mobile only rang once before he answered as Rebecca was mid gulp of her wine.

"Kitto, are you missing me or are you back in love with your mackerel?"

Kitto laughed. "There not paying for my fuel at the moment. I'm looking for a rich woman who wants to spend all day in bed with me and order take-aways, she should have a good figure and firm breasts. I'm thinking of putting an ad in the paper unless you know anyone that fits that description."

Rebecca blushed at the word firm, she'd not thought of herself that way but recovered and said "Kitto, I desperately don't want to push you into anything you don't want to do but have you ever thought of changing your job and lifestyle completely?"

"Only every winter when it's too cold or too choppy to go out in my small boat, and every summer when the mackerel catch gets smaller. Spring is quite nice though. I couldn't sell expensive property to rich knobs though if that's what you're going to suggest."

"Running a vineyard, walking among the vines talking to them, making wine that people actually want to buy?"

"I don't know Bec. I know about global warming and all that but in England it's still a dodgy thing to put your money into and when I say your money I mean it because any savings that I had have disappeared with diminishing fish catches."

"Okay. What if it wasn't in England? What if it was in South West France? What if I already owned the vineyard and it was already successful and getting even more successful?"

Rebecca felt confident enough not to wait for an answer to the first part and carried on to the point where the answer would have to be a definite yes or a definite no.

"Kitto, what if, on this end of the phone, I was down on my knees asking you to marry me. What if you knew that I wanted two children before I get too old to have any."

"Three"

"Sorry"

"I've always imagined us with three kids. Got names for them but you'd have to like them I suppose, the names not the kids. I'd say, very romantically, that I will be on the next plane to wherever you are but I can't afford the ticket. Can you wait for me to sell my boat and license? Am I rambling nervously? Have I mentioned I love you and this is not the old 'woman whose father owns a brewery' thing?"

"Yes you are rambling and no I can't bloody well wait. I want you now. I'll arrange the ticket and text you later with the details. I take it that without using the word yes, the word "three" means the same thing. I didn't tell you though that there is a condition."

"Ah, a catch."

"Not much of one. It's about our kids that you already have names for. I will speak to them, when you are not around, in Welsh. You must speak to them in English and make them respond in English. French they will pick up in the street and in school. I want them to be trilingual from an early age. You of course will have to learn a bit of French to get by with and to be able to understand your kids when they talk behind your back – which they will."

"Best day of my life and then you offer me French lessons on top of it all. I'll need them though, not looked at any of that stuff since reading Henri Bergson in the original French."

"We really need some time together to find out about each other. You keep surprising me and I have some huge surprises to tell you. Bye Kitto, I'll text you with your ticket details. Why don't you give your boat to one of your mates? Oh, and yes, you can choose the names as long as they're Cornish or Welsh names. Did I ever tell you that there's a Welsh version of your name? It's Gitto but spelt G-u-t-o."

"Your right, I'll choose the names, a git is something different where I'm from. Can't wait to be with you, wherever you are Rebecca Treseder."

"Sorry."

"Do believe you just proposed to a bloke you didn't even know the surname of. Do you do that often? You can keep your own name if you don't like mine."

"No, Treseder is fine, I was just in a world of my own." She lied and wondered how that had happened. He'd never been a person with a surname, he'd always been just Kitto.

The nice phone call over it was time to ring Para and she spoke to her in English also. "Para, can you talk?"

"Yes it is my day off and I am sharing an hour with Pedro. Not like you're thinking, you haven't interrupted anything but to let you know he is here and we have no secrets from each other. By the way he knows you are not gay now and says to tell you that you have destroyed his dreams for the three of us."

Rebecca switched to Greek and asked Para to put her phone on speaker. "Para, Pedro, I have a problem. You have invited me to your wedding in Greece with all your friends. I will invite you, one day to my wedding in France, I have proposed to Kitto and he has said yes. There is the problem. I have seen blue eyes, how did you call him Angelos, in France and worry that if I come to your wedding he will be there and is mad enough to kill me. Pedro has a new name and I guess no papers and will not be able to fly to France for my wedding. It is a big problem."

"Bec, I have you on speaker and we both heard all that. Can I discuss something with Pedro and ring you back?"

Walking around her cottage, kicking her heels, didn't take that long as it wasn't a big cottage. She imagined Kitto living there; she wondered what he would do all day once their exciting new love had cooled a bit, as all romances did. She wondered how good he was at building and whether he could convert the old barn at the end of the first field into a holiday let. She wondered if she really needed the income or the intrusion from a holiday let and whether she was using Kitto's hoped for building skills as a means to keep him from getting flabby and losing his muscle. She wondered if she was still being controlling.

Chapter 22

The laptop had already been set up with e mails and ticket orders for Kitto as if she was either clairvoyant or over confident. She moved to the other side of the kitchen table so that the screen was out of the glare of the early morning sunshine. The e mails were sent, as was the draft e mail to Geordie. It would be a shock for Geordie who was expecting nothing. He would receive, out of the blue, all the relevant photos and an explanation of how heroin was getting from Afghanistan to London and Paris, a description of the wine boxes and winery procedures, including what little details she had of the new owners, the address of the Paris flat and London restaurant and a short, follow up, e mail.

"Geordie, this may well be my last job. I am tired and should have taken the counselling. I need a rest, I need a life, I need to feel less weary."

Rebecca found the file she had constructed with all the other information from this case and extracted from it the photos from her memory card of the attempted victim burial, the photos that she had told Geordie would be valuable to the newspapers and, one day, may still be if extra money was needed. She returned to the case file. She had right-clicked the mouse and hovered the mouse pointer over the word "Delete." All of this recent effort to stop being in charge of her life, to stop being masterful, to stop having the upper hand, and there she was, accelerating in reverse gear, playing God, the ultimate controller. In her head she was not playing the one God that the Jews, the Muslims and the Christians all worshipped in their dangerously different ways. No, she was playing one of the Greek Gods of Paraskevi's Ancient Greek ancestors. The gods around her, sharing her cloud, looked like Kitto's ancient Greek philosophers.

Pretentiously she imagined she was a female God looking sage-like and powerful and surrounded by older men who were bald apart from a ring of curly white hair around the edge of their heads, each of the gods wearing a long white robe and looking down on the world at the characters as if studying chess pieces and deciding the next move and discussing the pros and cons with each other. It was most decidedly Rebecca's turn to make the next move; the other gods waited to see what she would do but were apparently unable to help her with her choice. To delete the files gathered there on her laptop would have huge consequences on this Earth that she was looking down on and was to be determined in a second by the movement of one finger.

If Rebecca sent this large file to Geordie then Monsieur Jeune would undoubtedly go to prison leaving Madame Jeune to bring up her two boys on her own as a one parent family. They had both taken a one-off risk that had not paid off as Rebecca had all their money. Perhaps Madame Jeune would go to prison as an accomplice. Then the two boys would go to family or into care.

Then there was Paraskevi. Was she the good friend who was trying to protect her lover at all costs, or had she known who was in charge of the drug running at the winery all along? She had definitely changed for the better but should she be left alone in her settled life, or catapulted back to a time when she was dominated by her father and his plans for her cousin-husband to be. The eight men of the island had spread themselves, and their ill gotten gains across the many islands that make up Greece and would hopefully spend that money in their local economies. They would be hard to now track down but it would be possible. Blue eyes was still angry but could never find out that the money he searched for was in Rebecca's safe. What if Petros was tracked down and jailed? Would it end the life of Para? How would the Greek Police feel about the fact that Paraskevi was his lover or even, by the time they caught up with him, his wife and that she was also the house cleaner of Rebecca who could be an accomplice?

All she had to do was to play God and press the button.

"So you see" Para's voice was still there on the other phone, had been partially ignored for the last ten minutes and Bec momentarily came down off her gods cloud, "I owe you so much. Knowing you and listening to your advice has changed me from the young woman afraid of her father and worried about marrying my cousin, into a confident woman who knows that I will have full control over my husband, with him knowing that I can reveal his past at any time. I owe you all this Bec and I thank you. We've cancelled our wedding for now so let me know what you think of our suggestion that we all marry on Cyprus as we can all get there and it would be nice for Pedro's friends not to have to return to their own island. Pedro says he will sort out Angelos and already has a story to appease him."

The call was ended with Rebecca promising to be at Para's wedding and wondering what Kitto would think about getting married on Cyprus, perhaps as a double wedding. She was not going to make the decision without him.

The brightly lit window in front of her provided a blank canvas for her thoughts. Her face without expression of any sort, her mouth open, her eyes lifeless. Perhaps the two women had been at opposite ends of a spectrum that ran from woman in charge of her life and other people's lives down to helpless trapped slave dominated by a father. Perhaps they had both moved to the middle of the spectrum. Perhaps they had crossed in the middle of that spectrum, perhaps they had even changed places. She held her breath, closed her eyes and pressed delete.

After a few seconds she looked at the screen, half expecting her laptop to be on fire. The computer hadn't believed her. "Are you sure you want to delete these files and all their contents?" It asked "Do you realise that you are differentiating between the bad guys you don't like and the bad guys you do like?" It seemed to add in her head. "Are you deleting these files to save yourself from enquiry when it's realised that someone has stolen the bad guys' money, making you the bad guy?" These words echoed around her head even though they were not on the screen.

"Yes" she screamed manically at the laptop and clicked on "Yes" at the same time. She was sure.

Rebecca stood up too quickly and found herself weeping with exhaustion and feeling light headed. Turning, she went to the living area and her bookcase and knew exactly the book she needed and which shelf it was on. She placed the book on the little shelf by the front door as she passed down stone stairs to her cellar, returning with a bottle of her own vineyard's red wine with the cork just pulled and a wine glass from the kitchen and placed both next to the book. Then she went upstairs to shower undressing as she moved towards the bathroom.

Her body moved constantly in order to catch the powerful jet of water from the power shower on all her body parts and it felt as though she was sand blasting a thin layer of skin that surrounded her. There was no shampoo used, there was no soap used, her idea was not to wash but to perform an act of cleansing. She tried to cleanse herself of the stench of murdering rapists, drug runners, people smugglers – all of whom had total control as their main objective – and to cleanse herself of her own controlling habits bred over a lifetime, the lifetime since Greg. Turning off the jet she let the water drip naturally from her body, her head against the tiled shower wall, listening to the drips hitting the shower tray. After a few minutes she stepped out of the shower but didn't towel herself dry. Reaching the bedroom wardrobe she found a very feminine, original 1980s floral pattern, Laura Ashley dress, bought from a dress agency and one that she hadn't worn for years having felt it too feminine for her matured character. Putting it over her head, she raised her arms which stretched her stomach and made her aware of the weight she'd lost through the weeks of walking, travelling and worrying, the showering ritual making her feel lighter still. The dress was allowed to fall to wherever it wanted to and she was pleased that it did actually fall. Her hair stayed inside the soft cloth and as she grabbed it to release it to the outside, the water from her hair, now cold, ran down her spine but didn't make her shiver. She retraced her steps, literally, following the wet footmarks on the timbered plank floor of the landing and then went downstairs. As she passed through the house door she picked up the bottle and glass in one hand, the book in the other and walked bare foot and underwear free across the yard, classical music playing in her head making it feel as if she was in a movie, then she seemed to float straight down through one of the long rows of vines in her vineyard. The soles of her feet were warmed by the sun-drenched, closely mown grass that had been allowed to grow in the strips between the vines. The roots of the grass were shallow but befriended the vines by retaining moisture in the ground that the vines would one day need when that moisture penetrated deeper. The deep and diving vine roots loved the poor soil they were in and thrived by finding moisture and minerals at great depths. Having walked on the grass Rebecca sat on it, lifting first the back of the dress to form a circle on the floor and to feel the warmth move from the grass to her bare bum cheeks and knowing that the patterns of the grass would make their mark there and on the backs of her legs. In anticipation of the autumn harvest to come, she stared at her vines, the stems of bunches formed but the small grapes not yet plump, not yet ripened by the sun that was slowly drying her hair and, as she stared, she thought of her own state, her inner body away from the sun aching for Kitto to take her into her autumn. She poured herself a glass of wine from the previous years vintage and under the hot sun opened "The Prophet" by Khalil Gibran. She had let go of the rope that held her boat at the harbour of controlling. The boat was slipping through the vineyard, into the Caudeau River, meandering eventually into the wide sea. She may be rescued by Kitto. She may be marooned on the desert island of her vineyard, growing old and producing a wine called Cuvée Spinster.

She opened the book and searched for the Prophet's teaching on marriage; a passage that she knew was there but had no reason to read previously. A phrase attacked her eyes, making her read it three times.

"But let there be spaces in your togetherness.

And let the winds of the heavens dance between you."

She felt that she was ready to share herself.

She felt that she was waiting for Kitto.

If you have enjoyed this novel and are interested in following Rebecca's further adventures through life then please visit;-

www.stephensonholt.com

You will be able to contact me to register your interest in knowing when the follow up novel will be released – with a promise of no spam.

Or at contact@stephensonholt.com

Again – no spam.

Thank you

Stephenson Holt @HoltStephenson

Made in the USA
Charleston, SC
30 November 2016